By the same author

My Name Is Michael Sibley
Five Roundabouts to Heaven
The Third Skin
The Paton Street Case
Marion
Murder Plan Six
Night's Black Agent
A Case of Libel
A Fragment of Fear
The Double Agent

GOOD OLD CHARLIE

An Inner Sanctum Mystery by

John Bingham

SIMON AND SCHUSTER
New York

CONTENTS

Part One
Launching Pad

1

*W*hen there is a return visit to a place, you are recording the actual visit, you are recording what you thought during that visit, and you are recording the events which produced those thoughts. A return visit is a blurred complex of fact and emotion. Above all, perhaps, of emotion.

They say you should never go back to certain places, on the grounds that if you have been happy there they will have changed, or friends with whom you dallied will have moved or died. Similarly, if the reverse is true, and you have been unhappy there, then why go back?

But I went back to Durrington in the end. Many years after I had left it, but I went back. I suppose I had to go back. It was a sort of challenge and at the same time I hoped it would be a catharsis.

I hoped I would finally shed the remains of the bitterness, sadness and fear associated with my involvement with Paul King.

Nobody who is not a native of the place, or has no special reason for returning, should ever wish to return to Durrington. It is a northern industrial town with red brick buildings, a gothic town hall, fuggy pubs and cobbled side streets which at one time used to ring with the sound of wooden clogs; depressing in winter, when the rain turns the dust on the pavements into coffee-colored slime, and not much better in summer, when the sun shows up the dirt on the walls and the grime on the windows.

The Council do their best, but a clock made of flowers, with hands that move, emphasizes rather than diminishes the surrounding ugliness. No town that was not ugly would need such an extraordinary contraption to cheer up the citizenry, or the passing traveler.

I left my car in the main municipal car park, and walked in the autumn sunshine to the side street where the Theatre Royal stood. There was nothing royal about the rickety building except the name. Here our Repertory Company had toiled away under the direction of Geoffrey Glover, surrounded by dust and indifference, concerned with the nuances of an inflection, the complexities of lighting, or the trembling of the blossom in the doomed Cherry Orchard, when all most of the population wanted was television, washing machines and electric mixers, in that order, though a minority, like Mrs. Daly, my landlady of that period, still liked a dose of Lilac Time, or Red Shadow and Desert Song stuff, at the Hippodrome.

I don't know why Geoffrey bothered to keep going, on his small grant from the Arts Council. Still, looking back, maybe I am seeing Durrington out of focus. Small wonder, really, in view of what happened. The seeds of greed, cruelty, treachery and tragedy were all there when I was one of the cast, and they had indeed flourished in the intervening years. Now I stood on the opposite side of the road, casually, under a tree, watching the cast come out for lunch, in two's and three's; some chattering and laughing, others, for whom the morning rehearsal had doubtless gone badly, looking silent and thoughtful. They were the cast of the current Repertory Company.

I didn't know any of them, and didn't expect to.

I only saw memories, ghosts, for want of a better word, like Vic Jones, kind and benevolent beneath his shrewd and truthful appraisal of people and things; too kind, too *truthful and uncompromising, to succeed in the theatre, or so it seemed to me; and with him were three youngsters, bit players, two girls and a boy, whose names I have forgotten. He always had youngsters round him, listening to his words of wisdom, sheltering beneath his veteran wings, for Vic was thirty-six if a day.*

Thus I watched the real cast without seeing them, seeing only these ghosts, and then only some of the ghosts, for I was holding back, deliberately prolonging the pain.

The ghost of Sarah Barnes came out, tall, gawky, like a colt, talking to Geoffrey Glover in his polo-necked sweater. Geoffrey was thin-faced, anxious, with deep lines down the side of his nose and mouth. Anybody who was producer of the Durrington Rep in those days had good reason to have a thin face with deep lines.

Suddenly Grace came down the steps, but she was no ghost. She looked stout and cheerful as usual. Her red hair had not lost its tone, the dye being as startling as ever. She used to tidy up and make cups of tea for us. She paused at the top of the steps, and I saw her head move in my direction and I raised the morning paper I was carrying, obscuring my face. On any other occasion I would have enjoyed a gossip with dear old Grace, a failed Rep girl who bore no malice, and wished everybody happiness.

But now I did not wish to quieten my heart, or dull the pain. Strange, but one is as one is, and when Grace had waddled up the street, there they were, coming out together, as I had so often seen them do—Shirley Baker and Paul King, the ghosts I had come to conjure up.

She was slim, brown-eyed, gazing up at him myopically, blinking in the daylight, radiantly happy at the prospect of eating a cheap sandwich with him, and drinking a half pint of thin beer.

Paul King wasn't looking down at her, glorying in her adoration, as I would have done. Not our Paul, not bloody likely. He always came out of rehearsal looking preoccupied and self-absorbed. He found himself a very absorbing subject.

9

The sight of Paul King, even the shadow of him, with Shirley, brought back a wave of my former jealously and resentment.

But I stood my ground for a few seconds. The emotion subsided. I turned away from the theatre, thinking now of other matters, such as the night Vic Jones telephoned me, just before midnight.

It was six weeks after the killing of Paul King.

2

On the night Vic Jones telephoned, I felt no sense of guilt about the actual killing of Paul King. You may declare that I was callous, remorseless, and treacherous. Maybe I was.

So was Paul King.

At least my love for Shirley was rooted in gentleness and protectiveness, right from the beginning, which was more than his feelings were. If I was a heel, so was he—a Third Form kind of argument, but ninety per cent of the world's citizens are basically Third Formers, stuffed to the remains of their evolutionary gills with atavistic lust, acquisitiveness, big hidden betrayal instincts, and little sordid ploys of ephemeral value.

If I am a cynic, show me a publicity agent in the entertainment world who isn't, and I'll take to the veil. The world will hold no more for me. I'll have seen everything.

Vic Jones had telephoned on the Friday evening. As a result, I slept little that night, and booked the following day for a couple of nights at the Spread Eagle Hotel, Midhurst, because I wanted to walk about the Sussex Downs, alone.

I had to get a grip on myself.

I left early in the morning, about seven o'clock, because I'd read somewhere that the police often pick you up around eight in the morning, and I had this sudden thirst for solitude, and clean fresh air, and the soft pastel shades of trees about to burst their buds. I wanted, as it were, to stock up against the days ahead. I had a lot to think about, too.

At first I thought I wasn't going to have my weekend. It is not easy to tail somebody at seven in the morning, without being spotted. I've worked out how it was done. I've had time enough.

There was a black Wolseley somewhere behind me as far as Roehampton. Then it disappeared, and was replaced by a dark blue Ford Zephyr, which was with me as far as Esher. Both were almost certainly Met police cars, highly polished, each with two men, and once, when I stopped for petrol, the Zephyr passed me but drew up in a lay-by some hundred yards ahead, while one man ostensibly looked for something in the boot. I think the Surrey police took over soon afterwards in a green Ford van, and subsequently the Sussex police, though by that time there were many cars on the road and I could not spot them with certainty. There was certainly a wireless link-up, and I believe that one car would drop me and wireless ahead to the takeover car.

At the Spread Eagle, in the light of what had happened on the way down, I telephoned my business side-kick, Jessie, at her home, saying where I was. She seemed surprised, but I made some excuse about coming in late to the office on Monday morning. It wasn't necessary, but I thought it might be handy later, to show I wasn't keeping my movements secret. A small enough card to play, but even small cards can break up a dicey interrogation and give you a few seconds to think.

During the whole of the weekend I noticed no obvious plain clothes officer keeping me under observation, but during a weekend many people come and go in the bars and dining room. The same goes for the Downs. Perhaps I was indeed under discreet observation. I don't know. If so, what did they expect to see me do? Bury something?

Like a pistol, for instance? How daft did they think I was?

So I walked the Downs, at times seemingly deserted save for sheep and an occasional little flip-wing bird, grappling with my distress and mounting fear.

But I still felt no sense of guilt about the actual killing. Not at that time.

It was six weeks since he had died, and I had been questioned and made my written statement, of course, and had been sure I was in the clear. Was I not known to be his close friend, his trusted publicity agent, the man who, as much as any man, had helped to build him up to stardom? Did I not owe my own rise in fortunes to him, and were not my future prospects in some measure linked with his continuing prosperity and good health? Had anyone ever heard me quarrel with him, even seriously disagree with him? Too true they hadn't! I'd made sure never to quarrel, all through the years.

Once I paused on the Downs, watching some sheep with my eyes, but in my mind I had a picture of myself in a witness box, ready to place my hand on my heart and say, with grim truth, "I can swear that from the day I met him till the day of his death, there was never a harsh word between Paul King and myself."

Two nagging questions worried me throughout that sunny weekend. Vic Jones had been questioned and asked to make a written statement about me. Why? He couldn't explain on the phone. Before ringing off he added that to his certain knowledge Sarah Barnes had also been questioned. Perhaps others. The police had harked back to the Durrington Repertory Theatre days, when we had all been actors together. Why?

I wondered who else had been questioned, and spent much time recalling the rest of the cast, conjuring up their faces, and in each case I was sure that I had revealed nothing of my plans. Yet in the back of my mind the lingering anxiety remained about the Durrington period. Else why, I kept asking myself, why have they delved back to those far off days?

What incident, what chance remark had been reported to the police? And by whom? It must have been an arduous task tracing the cast, now certainly dispersed about the country and even abroad.

I found no answer to my questions. I only knew that for some reason unknown to me Durrington was another way of spelling danger.

Paul King's end was violent, yet no violence was intended in my original plan. It often happens that way. A plan is evolved which, though devious, calls for no death or injury. Then, suddenly through the intervention of an unknown element, the scene is darkened and there is a shot, not even accidental but deliberate. Carnage and blood and splintered bone.

So it was with Paul King.

Yet such is the effect of sunshine after winter, and fresh air and exercise that I had calmed down and regained much of my confidence when I went to bed on the Sunday night. After a good dinner and a fair number of drinks afterwards in the bar, and a chat with a small round grocer who, like Jorrocks, also went fox hunting, I had come to the conclusion that if anybody was going to make a lot out of probably little or nothing it wasn't going to be me any longer. I even saw, with that clarity induced by two or three pints of beer and a couple of large whiskies, that the dark Wolseley, the Zephyr, the green van, and all the other cars on the road merely carried people setting off in good time for the weekend, like myself, or for a picnic.

I slept soundly with my door, as usual, slightly ajar. Some people lock their doors at night. I prefer a bedroom door not to be shut, let alone locked, like a cell door. In those days I got panicky if a bedroom door was locked, like a cell door. I've known myself get out of bed in the middle of the night to make sure the door was still ajar. I've grown out of it now.

There is no capital punishment in Britain, but there are endless nights of darkness and unreasoning panic for those in prison who are claustrophobic.

The next morning the sun was still shining and the air was warm. I spent the morning walking, then after a quick lunch I set out for London. I remember how good it felt to be alive and in reasonable health. I say reasonable health, because all the weekend, off and on, I had felt the onset of a cold. A slight tickling in the nose, a slight sore throat, and now and again a tendency to feel hot when the temperature of the room did not justify it. I hoped it would come to nothing, but on the run back the chill developed with unusual speed, and by the time I reached the West End of London I guessed I had developed a noticeable temperature.

I drove straight to the office, found a parking meter, and put in some money. I was turning away from the meter when a voice I knew said, "Good morning, sir. Detective Chief Inspector Williams' compliments and he wondered whether you could spare time for a few words with him, sir."

I turned round and saw Sergeant Ray and another plain clothes officer whose name I did not know, and don't know to this day. While I was putting money in the meter a black saloon car had slid up behind me. Nothing on it to say it was a police car. Driver in plain clothes. All very discreet. I had taken no notice.

Sergeant Ray was as I remembered him when I had made my statement after Paul King's death. Round face, fresh complexion, ginger hair, blue eyes. He had his hands in his beige overcoat pockets. He looked lean and tense, like a dapper ginger Tom cat which had just popped up from one of the basements.

"Now?" I said, hesitantly, and looked at my watch, not because I had an appointment but because it is the sort of thing one can do when one is surprised.

"If you don't mind, sir. He said to say it would be very helpful."

He had closed the distance between us, so that he was on my right. The other officer was at my left elbow. I felt a light touch on my left elbow, not a grip, more of a slight pressure towards the car.

"I ought to pop into the office," I protested.

"The Inspector said to say it was very urgent, sir."

"Then why isn't he here? He could have called at my office—"

"The Inspector's a busy man, sir," the Sergeant said.

"So am I."

"That's what he said, 'Mr. Maither's a busy man, there'll be interruptions at his office.' The Inspector said to say it would be better at the Yard. No interruptions."

The words were persuasive, but he looked challengingly at me.

"All right," I said, but before I'd said the words I'd felt a pressure on the other elbow and I was walking towards the black car. A sixth sense warned me it was better to go willingly.

They've got a new building now, overlooking Victoria Street. I suppose there was Scotland Yard, then New Scotland, and now there's a new New Scotland Yard, all tall and steel and concrete and glass and what have you. We were there in seven minutes, and nobody spoke on the way. I remember thinking how glad I was to have had my country interlude.

We didn't go to the Inspector's office. We went to a downstairs room, along a corridor covered with sound-deadening material, into a room with light gray walls. It was empty of cupboards. There was only a big table and a few chairs.

Inspector Williams was already seated at the table. He greeted me civilly enough and apologized for troubling me. All that codswallop. I sat opposite him, the Sergeant at the end of the table on my right.

The Inspector was heavily built, with a heavy rectangular face, close-cropped gray hair. He had a cleft chin and dark eyebrows. His face was gray. I think he was very tired.

His first words after the formal greeting made my heart

suddenly beat faster. A sort of sick feeling crept over me, and my lips felt dry. I licked them and tried to think above the drone of his words. He didn't look at me as he spoke, but I could see the Sergeant looking at me, sitting very still, with his alert, predatory Tom cat look.

The Inspector said, "The regulations say I must tell you that you do not need to answer any questions if you don't want to. If you wish to have a legal adviser present before you say anything, you are at liberty to do so."

"Look, let's get this straight," I said. "I've nothing to hide. And I'm not a barrack room lawyer, see? You say what you like to me, and I'll say what I like to you, right? I want to help, see? I'll sign something to that effect, if you like."

"You don't want to worry about that," the Inspector said.

"Nobody's charging you," the Sergeant said. "The Inspector here, he's not charging you with anything. He just wants some help."

"Listen," I said, "I know all about that line of talk. I know I can have a lawyer here if I want. I know all that, but I've got nothing to hide, see?"

You say that sort of thing off the cuff. It springs readily to the lips. I added, "So let's get at it. Let's clear it up once and for all. No holds barred."

The Inspector had been watching me with his heavy-lidded gray eyes. He said, "That's a fair offer, isn't it, Sergeant? You can't expect Mr. Maither to speak fairer than that, can you?"

"Fair enough," the Sergeant said.

His eyes weren't unemotional, like the Inspector's. They were hard and hostile. The Detective Chief Inspector was old enough, assured enough in regard to salary and pension, to want only the truth. The Sergeant wanted the truth, too. But I guessed he would press harder and faster for it than the Inspector. He had a career to make. Probably a young family to keep. He was the hunter. I'd said, no holds barred. He would take me at my word.

He said, "This statement, sir."

"What statement?"

16

"The one you made a few hours after Mr. Paul King's death, sir."

"Oh, that one."

"Yes, sir. That one."

The Inspector said quickly, "Mr. Maither might like to read it again."

"I don't need to," I said indifferently.

The sun was still shining brightly, then. No clouds on the horizon. But he pushed it across the table. After the usual preliminaries it said:

> I was Mr. King's publicity agent. I called on him short-ly after nine o'clock on the morning of his death to dis-cuss certain professional matters. He said he was going to Brighton for lunch with a Mr. Konzakis and other film people to discuss a film about Byron.
> He seemed in good spirits.
> Mr. King was a very close and dear personal friend, and had been since we acted together at Durrington.
> As far as I am aware he had no enemies. Our friend-ship remained unbroken when we came to London.
> He did not say he expected anybody else to call on him before he left. Our talk was friendly and about publicity for him. He was in good health and cheer-ful when I left him.
> I left at about nine-forty.
> I was shocked to hear of his death and do not know who could have caused it.

I tossed the statement back across the table to the Inspec-tor, and nodded, saying nothing. The Inspector said, "There's nothing you'd like to add or correct, sir?"

"It's okay as it stands."

"Bully for you, sir," said the Sergeant, cheerfully. "A lot of people want to change things later. They seem to have a kind of memory blockage when they're making a state-ment."

"It's natural," the Inspector said reprovingly. "It's natural, Sergeant. They're probably still flustered."

"That's right," the Sergeant said. "Still a bit flustered, some of them. But Mr. Maither, here, he was calm and composed throughout the interview, right?"

He looked at me, blue eyes still hard and hostile, and added, "That's right, isn't it, sir? You were calm and composed, you weren't flustered? Right?"

"More or less."

He had a notebook in front of him, one of those lined things with flip-back pages, and a crown, and something about H.M. Stationery Office on the front, and he was tapping it with a cheap, brown government-issue pencil.

He said loudly, "More or less? Either you were or you weren't flustered when you made the statement, sir."

"Everybody connected with a murder is on edge when they're questioned by the police."

He nodded, eyes still fixed unblinkingly on my face. The Inspector said, "The point is, Mr. Maither, you're not flustered now, six weeks later, are you?"

I shook my head.

"And you don't want to correct or add anything?"

I shook my head again and said, "That's my statement. I signed it. I've re-read it. I stand by it."

I hadn't been a professional actor for nothing. The Inspector picked up the statement again, gingerly, as though it was coated with poison. I didn't know what was eating him.

"It's like I said, Mr. Maither, you can have a legal adviser if you want one."

I sighed and said irritably, "You've told me that. What do I want a legal adviser for?"

"Look," the Sergeant said, sharply, "it's not for the Inspector to say what you may or may not need a lawyer for—the Inspector here, he's just pointing out you can have one here, now, while we talk, see?"

"Well, I don't want one."

The Inspector seemed to have a sudden idea. He pushed the statement at me and said, "Care to scribble that across the bottom—that you've re-read the above statement, you've nothing to add or correct at today's date, and you don't want legal advice."

But I pushed the paper back again, looked at my watch, and said, "I've got a business to look after. I came here voluntarily, at your request. Tell me how I can help you, and I will, and then I'll go. I haven't got all day you know."

I was forcing the issue because I was nervous. Silly, really. The Sergeant said quietly, "You said just now 'no holds barred.' We all say what we like, right? No complaints later, right?"

I nodded and put a light to a cigarette. The flame jumped when he suddenly said, very loudly, "Then you want to watch your step, you do. You don't want to get saucy with the Inspector!"

I was so taken aback I could only say lamely, "I wasn't being saucy. I just said I hadn't got all day. That's all I said."

"We have," the Inspector said, shortly. "After six weeks on this case, all day's nothing. We've got all day all right."

"And all night, too, if necessary," the Sergeant said. He stared at me with his round Tom cat merciless look, then at the Inspector and remarked mildly, "Must've been a nasty shock for Mr. Maither, sir—at nine-forty one morning he's got a close and dear friend and a business account, within about the next half-hour he's lost the friend and the account. Much money involved, sir?"

I shrugged, unable to see what they were getting at.

"I did his publicity for him on the cheap."

"Because he was a close and dear friend?" the Inspector asked.

"That's right."

"And his wife, you knew her?"

"Shirley? Of course. Nice girl, Shirley."

"Nice girl?"

"That's right. She didn't shoot him," I said, acidly.

"This unfortunate Mr. Paul King—if he was ill, would he tell the truth to his doctor?"

I looked at him in astonishment, and walked right into the trap, suspecting nothing.

"I suppose so. There's not much point in telling lies to your doctor."

"Might as well save your money," the Sergeant agreed, heartily.

"Do you agree with the Sergeant?" the Inspector asked, casually.

"Certainly I agree," I said without thinking, and almost at once felt my heart jump at the sound of a small alarm bell ringing in my brain.

"There's doctors and doctors," the Sergeant said. His voice was almost drowned now, by the sound of the ringing alarm bells. "There's ordinary doctors, homoeopathic doctors, gynecologists, bone doctors, psychoanalysts, psychiatrists—they all need to know the truth. Don't they?"

"Especially psychiatrists," the Inspector said. "If ever a doctor has to know the truth, it's a psychiatrist. Right?"

"Look, in a court of law—" I began, but the Sergeant wouldn't let me finish.

"Who's talking about a court of law, sir? All the Inspector here said was that if ever there was a kind of doctor to whom one would tell the truth, it's a psychiatrist. Right?"

"It depends what you mean," I said, fighting for time, sensing where the peril lay, hardly able to believe it.

The Inspector said, "The Sergeant means the truth. There's nothing complicated about that."

"Or is there?" the Sergeant asked.

"Or is there?" the Inspector repeated.

The Sergeant laughed and said, "Mr. Maither here, sir— he's a publicity agent, maybe his idea of truth is different."

"Not to a psychiatrist, it wouldn't be," the Inspector murmured.

The Sergeant agreed. "Not to a psychiatrist, sir. He wouldn't tell fairy tales to a psychiatrist. Waste of money."

Pride, fear of losing face, whatever you call it, is a dangerous thing. If ever a man needed a lawyer, I needed one now. I knew it. I didn't know what had happened. But I knew what was coming. Yet I didn't demand a lawyer, because I had twice said I didn't want one.

"You been to a psychiatrist, Mr. Maither?" the Sergeant asked, as if he didn't know. "You been to a psychiatrist lately?"

I nodded, fighting down the sick feeling.

"What was his name, sir?"

It was an automatic question. He obviously knew the name. His voice was unemotional. The hostile, triumphant light had died in his eyes. It was almost as if, confident that he had run his quarry to earth and could plunge the knife to the heart, the chase had lost its savor.

"Maynard, Dr. Maynard, of Harley Street," I muttered dully.

"Would you mind telling us why you consulted him, sir?" the Inspector asked, his voice almost gentle.

I said hopelessly, "I was mentally distressed, very distressed."

"Feelings of guilt?"

"I always thought that medical etiquette forbade—" My voice trailed away, but they knew what I was getting at.

I saw the Inspector and the Sergeant exchange a quick look. The Sergeant said brusquely, "Medical etiquette is one thing. Crime detection another. It is an offense to withhold information from the police which could lead to the detection of a crime, sir. Being an accomplice after the fact, right?"

I wasn't really listening.

I was thinking of Maynard, formerly Meyerstein of Vienna, lurking behind his desk, brilliant of reputation, but small, sallow-faced and old, the life juices seemingly drained out of him during the days of intrigue and the final flight from the Nazi terror. My mind was inside his mind, my thoughts were his thoughts, I was Maynard, formerly Meyerstein. I had built up a new career in a new country. I was naturalized, but a naturalization certificate can be withdrawn, and it is the duty of every citizen to help the police, and I, Maynard, cannot and will not be at odds with the law. I, Maynard, cannot afford to be.

Now, to my dismay, I felt my chill really beginning to come out. I felt my face begin to glow with the slight fever inside me, and knew that my forehead was becoming moist. The Inspector and the Sergeant stared at me. The Inspector woodenly, the Sergeant with feline attention.

The Inspector said, "What are you thinking about, sir?"

"Nothing," I said despondently. "Nothing much."

"Feeling all right? Anything the matter?"

"Feeling the heat?" the Sergeant asked. "Want the window open?"

"I've a feverish cold, that's all."

"Want the window open?" he asked again, and looked at the Inspector. "Perhaps the gentleman would like the window open?"

The Inspector nodded, and said, "Do you want the window open?"

I wiped my forehead with my handkerchief, and shook my head, thinking that if they mentioned the window again I would explode. The Sergeant said, "Perhaps the gentleman would like a glass of water?"

"Want a glass of water?" the Inspector asked.

I felt for a cigarette, and again shook my head.

"I'm all right."

"Sure you don't want a glass of water?" the Sergeant said. "Quite sure? You can have a glass of water if you want it."

I flung my cigarette packet down on the table and said loudly, "Thank you, I don't want the window open, and I don't want a glass of water. I'm *all right!*"

"Calm and composed?"

"Yes."

"Not flustered?"

"No."

The Inspector smiled at the Sergeant and said, "So we can go on, can't we? Make a note that Mr. Maither said he was suffering from a slight chill, but was otherwise calm and composed, and not flustered."

He had dark-rimmed spectacles for reading, which he whipped on and off as the occasion demanded. He had been re-reading my statement. Now he tossed it aside, whipped off his spectacles, and leaned across the table toward me, hands palm down on the surface.

He said, "You have nothing to add to this statement? No after-thoughts, nothing that has occurred to you during the past weeks?"

"I don't think so," I said slowly, to gain time. "I don't think I've anything to add."

They hadn't pressed me about old Maynard, and suddenly I was confident that nothing I had said to him could be used to pin the killing on me. I hadn't been such a mug as that.

"And no corrections you wish to make?"

"None," I said, firmly.

"To the best of your knowledge the statement is true in all respects?"

I nodded. Almost as I did so, I felt the dampness due to the fever beginning to gather again on my brow, and knew that my face was looking flushed. Again I took out my handkerchief and wiped my forehead.

They watched me, saying nothing.

I looked from one to the other, likewise saying nothing, thinking of Vic Jones' telephone call telling me that they had been questioning the old Durrington cast, still certain that I had never, in those far-off days, said anything to the detriment of Paul King, yet knowing that somewhere, somehow, I had slipped up.

They did not believe I had a chill. They thought that my periodically hot face and perspiration were due to fear, and when, later, I felt icy cold around the spine and shivered, though my brow still looked clammy, this merely confirmed their view. I was certainly afraid. I also had a fever. Too bad for me. They thought that my signed statement contained a fundamental lie. They didn't believe it.

In this they were correct.

Yet I thought that if I told them of the scheme I had evolved in Durrington, of the treachery and tenacity with which I carried it out until, all unplanned, it led to the deliberate shooting of Paul King, then I didn't think they would believe that, either.

3

Shirley was my girl, or so I had thought. And so did the rest of the Durrington cast, and so did Shirley, I believe, until I went away. Two weeks I was supposed to be away, that's all. I had a chance to pick up a hundred pounds or so for a bit part in a film down south, and, apart from the money, you never know what will happen if you get a toe in that racket.

Geoffrey Glover let me go without any fuss, which wasn't a compliment, but you can't have it all ways. In the event, I was away three weeks, owing to weather trouble, and when I came back Paul King had been installed for a fortnight, as the new young leading man, in place of Bob Brewer.

I'd known he was coming, but I hadn't worried. Why should I have done? Shirley had for me a sort of lost, vulnerable look. How was I to know that for Shirley, Paul had the same irresistible attraction? Three weeks I was away, that's all. Not that it would have made much difference even if I hadn't gone away. In some ways it might have been worse. Scenes and all that.

There was no "understanding" between Shirley and me, when I went away. By the time I got back, she'd just kind of slipped from me to Paul. No explanations called for. But in the days which immediately followed, when she caught me looking at her, I know that her gentle heart was saddened.

There was nothing she could do. I was short, with irregular features, older than Paul. I wasn't tall, slim and fair haired, with troubled dark-blue eyes and a little-boy-lost look.

I saw him for the first time at the rehearsal on the Monday morning after my return.

I came into the theatre with Geoffrey. We walked down the center gangway. The theatre was somber, only a work-

24

ing light on the stage, because it's no good wasting good juice on an Arts Council grant. We went up the temporary wooden steps to the stage, and Geoffrey introduced me to him. Paul looked up from his book. He was a great one for improving his mind, Paul was. He gave a wintry little formal smile and nodded. The reading began. They were taking on a play called *The Divided Heart*. Paul was playing the lead, a young man of weak character who was instrumental in disillusioning a young girl.

"Shirley, you read in for Sarah, she's at the dentist this morning. You'll be understudying her anyway," Geoffrey said.

Once again I felt the pang, as if something I had never believed could exist had come to life. Every affair I'd had seemed pointless. I sort of felt life could be beautiful. All very corny and, it sounds stupid to say it, but things I'd read about love again became true. I was standing like des Grieux in the courtyard, and I was watching Manon getting out of the coach.

It could have been her large eyes, luminous and weak the moment before she put on her glasses, or the curve of her breasts under her thin shirt, or the purity of her expression, or these and other things, not that anyone cares about purity these days. But purity shone out of her like a light from a torch. Well, maybe it did and maybe it didn't, but it did for me and that's all that mattered.

I suppose anyone else looking at her in that instant would just have seen a short, pleasant looking girl with large brown eyes and mouse-colored hair. When she started to read she put on her silver-flecked cheap plastic glasses; she was sitting next to Paul and her eyes were on him when I entered. She looked at me and smiled when I came in, but diffidently, without the blaze of welcome I had expected. I can't say my heart sank with dismay, but I was surprised and disappointed.

Geoffrey's voice calling my name brought me up short and I joined the cast, and the reading went on. As usual, I only had a small part.

It wasn't a very good play. But Geoffrey had to do some

sandwiching. If he plumped for the classics entirely, he would have emptied the theatre for good. He used to do the occasional sentimental piece, such as this one, or else a nice provincial comedy—run-of-the-mill Yorkshire pudding and gravy, to make the audience feel its heart was in the right place, and all that malarky.

We "broke" at eleven and went down to the basement for cups of tea. I found myself next to Vic Jones, who had also joined us in my absence. Vic was one of those good-natured actors everyone takes for granted, and consequently he usually got done down, either for laughs or jobs. He was tall, stooped a bit, and had a slight cockney timbre to his voice. He's still like that. This was awkward for him, like me and my ugly face.

"How do you like the Company?" I asked.

"Nice lot."

He could hardly say anything else, but Vic always looked on the bright side.

"Been in the business long?"

"Twenty years," he said.

A long time, too long, and we both knew it. The theatre is like the winnowing floor of the granary, the light chaff is easily dispersed. Only the real grain survives. And some people, long after they have become mildewy, still hug their illusions, hanging around theatre clubs and agents' offices, telling themselves that so-and-so was forty before he got a break, that such-and-such made good in TV at fifty. We knew the form, but neither of us was letting on. We weren't displaying our sores, but we each knew the other thought he was too old to be still in Rep, and we each knew the other was right.

At lunchtime, Vic and I walked down the cobbled alleyway to the Builders' Arms. Paul and Shirley were walking in front of us. She wore a white blouse and skirt. She was looking up at him, and he seemed to reply in monosyllables, taking it all for granted, that and his good looks. Some people have it made.

By the time we got to the pub, Paul was sitting on a bench in the far corner, and Shirley was fetching him beer and sandwiches from the counter. Vic said, "A pint and a cheese sandwich? Bitter?"

I nodded, and handed Vic the cash. The bar was very crowded. I was watching Shirley in the mirror, the way I watched her the day of the wedding.

When Vic came back I jerked my head in the direction of Paul.

"What's he like?"

"Nice boy, but he wants it all at once."

"Good actor?"

"He will play it for sympathy."

We both knew that that meant hogging the act. But that was the way Paul was. He wasn't a mucker-in.

Not like Sarah Barnes. She played all the leads with Paul. And she hated him, as I discovered later. She said he was a bad actor, sometimes in his hearing, which didn't make things cozy in the company. Sarah had come up the hard way. Her parents had been unsuccessful music-hall performers, and she had an overriding ambition to get her own back on the world. She wasn't good looking, and later used to say Shirley was Paul's toffee apple.

"He hasn't got enough guts to stand on his own bloody feet! Has to run back to Momma for comfort," she'd say.

Sarah and I had a lot in common.

We hadn't been rehearsing for more than a couple of days when I got Paul's measure. Vic was right about him. He was playing the part for sympathy, throwing the play off balance. Geoffrey was patience itself, though on one occasion he stopped rehearsal in Paul's scene and said irritably, "No—here you've got to give the impression you think she's young and stupid—*humiliate* her!"

Paul shrugged his shoulders and looked down with a half smile on his face. Not superior, just detached, knowing better, not saying it.

Vic and I were sitting in the wings on the first night. We'd got quite chummy by this time.

"He's mucking Sarah's part," Vic muttered, "but the audience will like him."

We didn't say anything else. We didn't need to. When we

went round to Sarah's dressing room, after the first night of the show, she was in tears of rage, walking up and down. Sarah was a tall girl. A good five foot seven. Height is a nuisance for an actress. No good making your leading man look like a dwarf, if you can avoid it, but sometimes you can't. Not that Sarah did, but she had straight, severe features, and black hair, which didn't always help. It's a hard enough struggle for actresses, anyway, even if they're not too tall. No one seems to realize that there are fifty per cent more parts written for men than women. Paul always managed to make her look gawky if he could. There are lots of small ways you can throw people off balance.

"He's a sod!" said Sarah, after the first night performance.

Vic was sitting on the edge of her dressing table.

"You were fine, ducky," he said.

"You can't fool me, I was terrible!"

"Far from it," I said, backing up Vic, "You were—"

"No, I wasn't!" she snapped.

"You were fine!"

"No, I wasn't!"

It went on in this childish way for a while, and then stopped. We had to dress our wounds and get up to the bar. Civic reception, a new red-faced fat Mayor, speeches, gins and tonics, stodgy sausage rolls, and all that.

I went up and congratulated Paul. Mostly because Shirley was standing next to him, and I wanted to be near her.

"You need to judge the local audience," Paul said.

"Wasn't Paul wonderful?" Shirley said.

Her lips were parted. I remembered their softness, I had only kissed her twice.

"He certainly was good," I said carefully.

I turned and murmured a further conventional phrase of congratulation to Paul, though the words stuck in my throat. I could have saved my breath. He obviously didn't hear me. He was staring down at Shirley with a fixed, almost glazed expression, as though for the first time he was realizing her potentialities, as though he was recalling Geof-

28

frey Glover's words, "You've got to give the impression you think she's young and stupid—*humiliate* her."

He didn't humiliate her then, of course. He just stared down at her with his somber, dark-blue eyes, sort of speculatively, and, as far as I recall, that was the first time I was conscious of a feeling about him which made me uneasy. It was gone in a flash, and nothing remained but professional dislike and normal male jealousy. Quite enough, for a start.

Shirley obviously felt nothing but adoration. He hadn't made passes at any of the other girls in the cast, he hadn't slept around with them, though I expect he could have done. To her it made him seem the young Sir Galahad he looked.

I know, now, why he had not tried his luck with the other girls, and it wasn't because he had homosexual tendencies. Far from it. In some ways it might have been better if he had. It would have saved two deaths—possibly three, give a death take a death. Shirley would not have married him. But she did.

They were married at Durrington Registry Office, between shows, on a Saturday. For better or worse.

Shirley was wearing some sort of tweed suit and blouse. Blue, I think it was. It was too big for her. She had that nervous look she always had in theatre. As if she'd lost some of the props. She wasn't wearing her glasses, and looked more vulnerable than ever. Geoffrey Glover had the ring in his pocket and handed it over at the right moment. I could see the whole wedding like shots in a film; Paul looking the way he always did when playing the young juvenile, fair hair, blue eyes slightly open with that "youth surprised" look he did so well. Shirley's hand trembling a little; perhaps she was frightened, or maybe it was joy.

Shirley had lost her parents in an air crash some years before. Paul's mother, Edith, was there. His father, according to Paul, had been a drunk, had nipped off during the war, and never returned, and personally I didn't blame him, having seen Edith. You couldn't say relatives were in good supply, and the one who was there, Edith, looked about as approving as a diner who has found a hairpin in his soup.

After the wedding we went round to drinks at the Builders' Arms. All the company were there being jolly-jolly and convivial, like the first act of *Trelawney of the Wells*. I was smiling, and went on smiling till my face ached. I was thirty-five at the time, and felt sixty-five. I could see Shirley looking at Paul in the mirror behind the barmaid's head. When we were making up I used to watch him in the glass in the same way. I knew every line on his face. Although he got all the best parts, he always had a grumble. He knew just how to discourage people, too. If you got a good part, he would point out how stupid the play was. If the play was good he'd say, "Shame they're not using you this week."

I thought I knew why Paul was marrying Shirley. I was partly right. In addition to that other thing, about which I knew nothing for sure, he wanted someone who thought he was a genius. Kean and Garrick rolled into one. She thought it all right, and it gave him a shot in the arm. Talk about a disciple, she could have doubled for the whole twelve.

I slipped away when the wedding party started to get noisy, made some excuse and went back to the theatre. Anyway, I hate playing when I'm muzzy.

It was a pretty crummy old theatre, as I've said; though the Arts Council had done the auditorium up a bit, the basement was full of rotting settees. It smelt of old plays, of disappointment, of final curtain calls, the echo of dead applause, and the mustiness of fading hopes.

I sat down on a broken settee, and looked at a spotted picture of Ellen Terry. Geoffrey Glover, next door, was chatting up Grace, who made the tea. I heard her say, "I bet they made a sweet couple."

I went on staring at Ellen Terry though I could hardly see her. I comforted myself with the thought that tear glands are made to be used.

My trouble as an actor was that I didn't look right. I knew this and so did Geoffrey. My voice is good, but I'm too short, and my face is ugly and when you're an actor you don't only have to sell your voice, you have to sell your face, your gestures, and the way you move. I had nothing to sell except my voice. It's a nasty feeling—knowing that you can do something, feeling inside you the engine which could drive forward, yet knowing that the chassis is not up to standard.

Geoffrey would never have told me this; he didn't need to, and I think he knew it. Oddly enough, in some ways, I often felt that Geoffrey and I were on the same beam about Paul. As a producer he was shrewd enough to know most of Paul's faults, but often in productions he would mask them, letting Paul have his head so that his confidence wasn't destroyed. Confidence is a frail flower, a touch of frost and it's gone.

One trick Geoffrey missed, or chose to ignore, about Paul was his selfishness as an actor. But then he wasn't acting with him. He didn't have to put up with Paul pinching the best laughs in comedy by upstaging, or giving the occasional unscripted sob in tragedy, which spoilt an entrance.

Paul was twenty-five when he joined us. He struck me as type cast for a poor Russian student, or one of Rodolphe's chums in *La Boheme*. He hadn't got a modern face, I thought, and, though he laughed easily, he always had this thoughtful, unhappy look behind his eyes, as if he'd had bad news from home. This went down very well with the girls, including Shirley. They longed to comfort him. Went down well with the local audiences, too, though that was where Geoffrey missed another trick about Paul. Paul wanted the audience to love him, and used them as salve to his ego. There's a difference between that and being great as an actor.

To an actor an audience is a living entity, like an animal to be tamed: "They were easy tonight . . ." "They were hard to get going this afternoon—Christ, what a matinee, it died the death! . . ." "What the bleeding hell happened in Act II?—they just weren't there at all . . ."

"*They*"—anonymous, amorphous, faceless, and yet giving out a feeling which is necessary and vital to the actor, and to the success of the play. After a while Paul had got the Durrington audience tamed. He knew just what he could get away with, and he despised them for it. It was too easy.

4

It was inevitable that during that return to Durrington, after all the years, the bitterness, the tragedy, that my thoughts should be scattered, flashing to and fro in time. Although for a while my memories might be of the place itself and all that had happened there, in the next instant they were concerned with Paul King's killing, the aftermath, the police investigations and how, during my last interrogation, I had so desperately tried to recall where I had made a mistake in the Durrington period.

Thus the return to Durrington evoked memories resembling the layers of an onion. I was recalling the period and I was recalling how I had tried to recall the period when under interrogation. I have said that I felt no sense of guilt at that time. Nor did I. The remains of hate and jealousy, yes, and bitterness, too, but no guilt.

For guilt can creep upon you slowly and stealthily, sometimes in the night, which is understandable and sometimes, unexpectedly, in the quiet countryside, when you question whether you have a right to enjoy the sunshine and bird song.

Therefore, during my return to Durrington I had to resist the desire to push back the ever-searching questions, the probings, the secret uneasiness, the nagging worry that self-deception and specious excuses, rich, mature and well padded, had concealed mere animal lust and professional jealousy, and promoted a line of action which lead to death for Paul King.

I searched as truthfully as I could in the end, hoping that that which I feared would not be there, yet afraid that it would.

From the Theatre Royal, I wandered on foot to the Registrar's Office, where the desultory wedding of Shirley and Paul King had taken place and then, inevitably, to the depressing street where Paul King and I had lodged.

They went off after the Saturday show on the day of the wedding, and didn't come back till the Monday evening. I think they spent a couple of days somewhere in the Dales.

Personally I laid in some gin and whisky and spent most of those two days plastered, in my bedroom. All very corny and I told Mrs. Daly I had 'flu. She didn't believe me, because her husband drank like a fish, and she knew the symptoms.

I felt grim on Monday. It was a good job that I had such an undemanding part in the play. This was partly because it was one of Geoffrey's sweetness-and-light weeks, and he was doing *French Without Tears*. I hated the play, and was playing the corny French father part complete with beret and velvet coat. I didn't look the part. Couldn't do the accent, either. Paul drew my attention to that. Kind of him, especially as I'd just forked out £ 2 for a wedding present. Made all the difference to my performance.

The whole of the weekend I was dreading Monday night.

Paul and Shirley had taken the two top rooms in Mrs. Daly's house, and my room was beneath theirs. They'd turned Paul's old room into a sort of sitting room, and bought themselves a double bed for the other room.

I couldn't sleep for a long time on the Monday night. I'm not given to erotica usually, and I don't think I have a voyeur streak, but every ordinary old creak of the floor boards was agony. It is easy to say I should have moved before they were married, but they'd kept their plans secret till the last moment. It's the sort of daft thing people do.

Two days later I did move because I couldn't stand it any more.

"Rep" sounds tatty and it very often is, but in Durrington we did at least run the plays for two or three weeks, and that meant rehearsing the new play while we were acting the old one. It wasn't so bad, at least you had time to "build" your performance a bit, whereas in weekly Rep you only just have time to learn the lines.

There was not the "night of the long knives" feeling you get when a commercial management has ten thousand smackers at stake. It's a bit frantic then. Money is a serious subject, very serious. But in Rep some were young, and opportunity seemed just around the corner, and all I can say is, it's a good thing we can't see round corners.

It was about this time, ignorant of any other weapons which I might or might not have used, that I began to conceive my long-term plan to wreck the marriage, and catch Shirley in my loving arms as she fell out of the debris.

Extraordinary as the plan was, it gave me a sense of hope. More, it gave me a feeling of power and, above all, an outlet for my hatred of Paul King. I felt that though he seemed to be the winner, I was, in reality, manipulating him.

Like many operations, notably during a war, when some plans succeed and others fail, it was based upon many hopeful possibilities and a few basic facts.

First, was my diagnosis of Shirley's feelings. These were based, not only on Paul's good looks, but upon the little-boy-lost air, which he could switch on at will, and upon his undoubted need for moral support in his career. This "being-in-need-of-care-and-attention," as the police call it, was something which no woman with Shirley's maternal instincts could withstand for long.

Second, was my diagnosis of Paul's character, aided by the fact that we shared a dressing room, a sordid enough room where we still had tin bowls on legs to wash in.

I knew the role he had cast for me. Charles, His Friend. Good old Charlie, who'd taken the loss of his girl in good part. Dear old Charlie, he'll never let you down. We had some cozy sessions in that dressing room, as I watched him in the mirror, pretending not to be looking at him. He had a habit of looking at himself, very seriously, examining his face, making sure of the best angles. It was quite an experience, listening, getting his measure, understanding the deep-rooted self-absorption which lay at the center of his character, and the contempt for other people. Most people are flawed. It helps, when you want to strike, to know where the flaws lie.

I'm not pretending it wasn't hard listening to the crap he talked, and going on about Shirley and what a help she was to him, how she was a natural when it came to intonations, and how she heard him his lines every single day. And hearing all about the confidence she gave him, and how an actor needed someone to believe in him if he were ever going to do anything worthwhile.

The only times the cast got frantic was when one of the London managers was "in front," talent-spotting. Geoffrey wasn't against this. He liked his actors to show their paces, and it isn't always the best talent that gets on the boards in London. I knew that Geoffrey thought Paul needed another two or three years before he hit London. But Paul was impatient for a chance. I wanted it for him, too.

I will repeat that, loud and clear: I wanted Paul to have a chance and not merely a chance. I wanted him to seize that chance with both hands and, with all the selfishness and conceit of which he was capable, which was unlimited, I wanted him to climb the ruthless ladder of fame and fortune.

The end, when he lay in his own blood, was no part of the original plan.

In those early days in Durrington, when I was nurturing my hate and jealousy, I had a single aim in view. The road to it would be tortuous and painful but I had little doubt about the outcome.

I wanted Paul King to be a star.

There was an element of risk. It was not that he would eclipse me in the theatre, that was inevitable, it was what would happen if the balloon of his conceit and ambition were to be punctured.

If he failed, Shirley would stick to him through thick and thin. But if he succeeded, if he became a star, what then? She would rejoice, but what of Paul? Would Paul stick to Shirley? Therein lay the gamble, and I thought the odds were on my side.

It would not be enough if he were to be only moderately successful, earning a reasonable income and always sure of a job. He had to become a star. I would not begrudge him his wealth. He would be welcome to it.

All I wanted was his wife.

Strange and farfetched though it sounded, the plan seemed to me to be eminently logical.

A man shoots to stardom and with him, happy and excited, believing that virtue and merit is at last being rewarded, is the wife he married when they were still struggling to survive at ground level. Perhaps she is a simple, untalented girl, not over-burdened with brains, or wit, or social graces, or poise, or even, come to that, good looks. Still, Flossy is good enough to cook, comfort and encourage and all the rest of it. This being a just world, Flossy is at last rewarded. Well, isn't she? She must be, mustn't she?

Don't make me laugh.

Flossy is paid off, ditched, lucky to get her check. To our hero sophistication has come with success. Nobody could call Flossy sophisticated, or even particularly young looking any more, and no wonder.

Bye-bye Flossy, and no hard feelings.

I'd seen it happen over and over again. The first casualty in the rocket rise was the wife. All right for starting fuel, then shed, like the rocket booster.

Nevertheless, if Shirley had shown signs of being radiantly happy during the first weeks of the marriage I do not think I would have acted as I did. But she didn't.

Some days, about one in ten, she looked like the cat that's drunk the cream. Most of the time she looked kind of neutral. Now and again downright miserable. Vic noticed it, of course. One day, over lunchtime cheese and beer, he said, "Lover Boy looks like a mixed blessing for Shirley."

"Marriage teething troubles," I said.

Vic took a gulp of beer.

"Me, I didn't have any of those. I just broke my teeth later. She nipped off with an American Air Force sergeant."

I stared at him in surprise, not knowing he had been married.

"I'm sorry," I said. He laughed.

"I'm not. I sent her a greetings telegram saying, 'Come back, nothing is forgiven.'"

If anybody else in the cast noticed anything, they said nothing to me. I speculated on what the teething troubles were, thinking they were caused by their different characters, hers gentle and loving, his selfish and self-absorbed. I was only partly right. Yet the information was there, though not exactly for the asking. One day, when we were alone for a few moments in the wings I had the temerity to say to her, "Everything working out all right with Paul?" It was courting trouble.

"What do you mean?" she snapped. It was the first time I had seen her irritable.

"What I say," I muttered lamely. "Just asking, that is all. Polite question, that's all."

"Why shouldn't things be working out all right?"

"No reason—no reason at all."

"Well, then!"

"Look," I said, miserably, "I'm fond of you. You know that?"

"So what?"

It was a defiant, rude, even callous question.

She wouldn't have said it if she had been happy. It told me all I wanted to know.

"So nothing," I said, and made to turn away. But she put a hand on my arm and stopped me.

"You people—you don't understand Paul."

"What people?"

"The cast—and you," she murmured sadly. "You see him as selfish, self-absorbed—it's because you don't understand him, you don't understand what it is to burn with a hard, gemlike flame."

I stared at her aghast.

"To burn with a *what?*"

"Hard, gemlike flame," she repeated seriously, and I suddenly realized that because she was so young she could not appreciate the enormity of the cliché she had used.

"I suppose not," I said. "I suppose that's it, I suppose he is consumed by a hard, gemlike flame."

"He is!"

"Ah!"

I didn't know whether to laugh or cry.

"At times the frustration of Rep work in Durrington overwhelms him. And then he—"

She stopped, but having got her that far I wasn't going to let her off the hook.

"And then he—what?"

"Oh, he says all sorts of things he doesn't mean. Hurtful things. Like all real artists he's *temperamental,* he doesn't *mean* them."

"I'm sure he doesn't mean them—"

"I know he doesn't," she said with certainty. "I know it for sure, because when he sees he's pained me he is suddenly—all tenderness. Loving and wonderful," she added dreamily.

I was hardly listening, because I remembered Geoffrey Glover stopping the rehearsal that day, and saying, "You've got to give the impression she's young and stupid. You've got to *humiliate* her." I also remembered the curiously speculative look in Paul's eyes which I had seen when he gazed down at her during the reception we gave to the new mayor.

I thought I understood why he had not been particularly attracted to other girls in the cast, or, if he had given them a passing thought, why he had passed them over in favor of Shirley. She was the gentlest. She was the easiest to hurt. She was the most vulnerable.

Makes you think, really. He fell for her because she looked vulnerable, and was; and she fell for him because he had the little-boy-lost look, and seemed vulnerable, and wasn't.

And me? Nobody fell for me in Durrington. I didn't look

38

vulnerable. Never did. Never have been. I've always been keen to fight back. One way or another.

I guessed then what I know now. Paul King had to hurt the girl to whom he wished to make love. Not necessarily hurt her physically. Humiliation, degradation would do. Anything which made her whimper. Psychologists will give you the answer. Maybe I should say psychologists will give you the answer which satisfies psychologists. I've got my own crude remedy for people like Paul King, and others, too, come to that. Not *all* psychological cases, mind you, but a good many. It's a cheap remedy, too, consisting of a dose of salts, a kick up the backside. Maybe I never was suited to play sensitive parts in the theatre.

It seemed to me then, as it seems to me now, having weighed the evidence, that I was justified in going ahead with my plans.

One evening in the dressing room, Paul King said, "I'm fed up with this bloody town."

I was looking at him in the mirror, watching his expression. He wasn't watching mine. Just as well. It was the opening I had been waiting for.

"Why don't you send some of your cuttings to Reg Taylor?" I asked. Sort of casually, as though it was a passing thought.

His hand paused in the act of wiping off some make-up. I saw him thinking over the idea, weighing the risks.

"Geoffrey wouldn't like that," he said.

"Why should he know? I know a chap in Reg's London office. I could send them for you."

He looked at me in surprise. It's not often people actually rush forward to do you a good turn, like I was doing.

"Reg is always on the lookout for people," I added mildly.

I knew why, too. He didn't have to pay "discoveries" so much money. He's a bit out of favor, since the rise of the *avant garde,* but some years ago he was very powerful indeed.

I could see my own honest, cheerful face in the mirror,

looking pleased that a friend might get a break. For a moment he looked suspicious.

"Why should you help me? Why don't you write about yourself?"

I shrugged my shoulders.

"Sending what cuttings?" My tone of voice conveyed a sort of bad luck for me, good luck for you, Buster. After all, I was an actor. Of sorts.

"He might give you a job. You never know," I said.

"That's too much to hope."

He was doing the modest boy act he sometimes did with Geoffrey.

"You know you're good," I said earnestly.

He did, too. So I wrote off. Decent of me.

Two months later I went into the dressing room. I wasn't on until the second act, and I'd been studying my part for the following week. For once I had something reasonable to do. Paul was sitting at his mirror. He was playing the John Gielgud part in *Musical Chairs*. It's an old play, but Geoffrey liked it, and Paul could play the piano. I think Geoffrey chose it to give Paul a chance to do a nice canter to the winning post with the audience. There's nothing like that doomed pianist bit to get them sobbing in the aisles.

"Reg Taylor's in front," muttered Paul.

"Sarah told me."

We laughed. Perhaps neither of us had seriously thought anything would come of my letter. The bait, such as it was, was unripe, immature and not over-filled with juice, but probably more promising than some. Reg decided it might be worth digging tentatively into his jeans. He took the bait. For one thing, the piano playing bit went down a treat and, for once, the lighting was good. Focused right on Paul's fair hair.

After the show, Paul and I went down the cobbled alleyway towards the Grand Hotel. He was going to have drinks with Reg.

We left the theatre together, but after a few yards I tagged discreetly behind, leaving him to go down the narrow lane alone. We used to call it the Triumphal Way, because it was always trodden by those summoned to a talk by a visiting London manager. But it was a two-edged name, born of a sort of schoolboy irony. There weren't only the victors in a Roman Triumph. There were the prisoners, the victims, those destined, in due course, to be slaughtered. Probably the nickname was rooted in jealousy and latent ill-will.

Me? I was filled with jealousy and stuffed with ill-will. But I wished him success. If ever a man trod the Durrington Triumphal Way with a heartfelt blessing, it was Paul King. Two blessings, because Shirley was standing in the shadows, watching him go. She was looking at him as if he were a vision from heaven. She put her hand on my arm.

"He must—*must* give Paul a break."

"I hope he does," I said fervently. "By God, I hope he does!"

"What do you think?"

"I feel he will."

"Do you really think so?"

She looked beautiful, eyes shining, lips parted, pale, and the hand she put to her hair was trembling with excitement. I said abruptly, "Let's go and have supper at Dino's."

"You can't afford it."

"No, but it might be a great day."

Looking back on it, Dino's was a pretty tatty joint, but on a gray night in a northern industrial town it seemed quite Continental. You could get Spaghetti Bolognese for five bob for two, and we had a bottle of red wine.

I admit there were occasions when I found the situation almost untenable, and one of them was that dinner. I would like to say that I looked back on it with warm, sentimental feelings, recalling how Shirley's mere presence made the filthy brown soup almost palatable, and the glow of her personality lent added flavor to Dino's spaghetti from which, that evening, I swear even the dogs of Bologna would have recoiled in disgust.

Not so. There were occasions when waves of nausea swept over me which were not caused by the food. I will draw aside the veil only sufficiently to report that there were lengthy, seemingly unending passages devoted to Paul's talent, overt, latent, past, present and potential. Others devoted to breaks he should have had, didn't get, might get now, and should get in the future. Others again were devoted to his vibrant delivery, his figure, and his face, head and hair, viewed from the front, in profile and even from the back.

I must frankly admit that that evening, and indeed to a greater or lesser degree throughout that period of her life, dear, gentle Shirley was rather a soppy date. There was a tinge of the milch cow in her. In me, the trait aroused protectiveness, in Paul, other things. It was not a trait which was destined to last. In the circumstances, it couldn't.

The only part of the dinner I enjoyed was towards the end. She began again, tediously, repetitiously and vehemently, "Paul can't go on and on in Rep! He *must* get a break soon!" Then she added— "Wasn't it wonderful luck Reg Taylor coming down like that?"

If it had come at the beginning of dinner, I would have been able to ride it. Coming at the end of an evening of all that soppy adulation, it was more than flesh and blood could stand.

"No, it wasn't lucky," I said crisply.

"What on earth do you mean?"

She looked hurt and flabbergasted, like a thrush that has suddenly been mauled by a passing worm.

"What on earth do you mean?" she repeated.

"I mean I wrote to Reg's office and sent them some of Paul's cuttings."

"You did that for Paul?"

"I did it for both of you," I replied, and glanced down modestly at my plate. "Don't tell Paul. Let him think rumors of his talent have reached London." I was damned sure Paul wouldn't tell her himself. "Better for his self-confidence. Anyway, it was Paul's acting tonight that counted," I added, thinking of the choice of the play, the piano, the lighting which was exactly right. She took the fly eagerly.

"Oh, yes, I know that, of course."

Even in her besotted state she must have felt that something more was required. She leaned across and put her hand over mine, saying nothing, indicating that never, never would she forget my kind deed. She was an actress, after all.

"He is my friend," I murmured simply. "And you know how I feel about *you*."

"Dear Charlie!"

I gave a sad, brave, tumbril smile, indicating that it was a far, far better thing that I had done, than I had ever done before. I saw her home. Paul was waiting for us, and gave us a warm welcome.

"Where the bloody hell have you been?"

Shirley's eyes filled with tears.

"Charlie took me out to dinner." She looked at him nervously, almost in anguish, and added miserably, "Did you get the job?"

Paul shrugged angrily.

"I don't know, and I'm not used to large gins, not on my salary, and I feel plastered—I haven't had any supper."

Paul always kept the essentials in view. He wasn't worried about me taking Shirley to supper, only about her not cooking his. I made myself scarce. I could see that this was not a time for cracks, and went back to my digs. Cold it was, too, and my new landlady had fixed it so that a shilling in the gas only lasted three-quarters of an hour, not long enough to get the damp off the walls.

I put on another sweater and climbed into bed.

In the morning I usually picked up Shirley and Paul and we'd walk to the theatre together. I didn't see Paul the next morning. Shirley was in the kitchen cooking herself bacon and eggs. I think she felt bacon and eggs might cheer her up. The way I thought a bottle of whisky might cheer me up on the wedding night. They never do, of course, but it's a nice thought.

No need to ask Shirley what was the matter. I could see Paul had been doing his Hamlet bit most of the night. Not that I thought he could play Hamlet. But I'm certain he got full value out of the part when he was in bed with Shirley. It must be difficult playing Hamlet in bed but I'm sure Paul managed it. Some people act much better off stage than on.

To the relief of all concerned, including me, Reg Taylor did offer Paul a job in a play which was going out on tour, and then, of course, "straight into the West End." They always are.

"What do you think?"

Paul was looking at me in the mirror, after the offer arrived, asking my sincere advice.

"This is a big chance, but supposing the play packs up—and doesn't hit London?" he asked.

He was weighing up the pros and cons. Sixty a week for a month's tour was good gravy, but what happened if you found yourself out on your ear afterwards? London is a cold place for out-of-work actors.

"Geoffrey doesn't think I ought to do it."

He looked at me again. For once he was uncertain. He wanted a good friend's judgment on the problem.

I felt a wave of alarm. Just when the rocket was going to get off the launching pad it looked as if it might develop a last minute hitch. This wouldn't do at all. But I had to play it cool. None of your rumbustious slaps on the back and boisterous, meaningless reassurances.

"Geoffrey would naturally think that," I said slowly. "After all, he has got an angle. You're a draw with the local audience."

Paul was making up. He looked at me again in the mirror. I could see that slight lowering of his eyelids when he was thinking something out.

"I think you're right," he said, smoothing out his make-up.

He looked better brown. A little No. 9, or a touch of pancake, gives that healthy outdoor glow on stage which actors rarely have off it. Off stage, they often look like underdone suet puddings.

"You're right," he said, looking at himself seriously. "I *am* a draw."

44

"You wouldn't be easy to replace."

He considered that, too, and agreed with me. The following week, when casting for *Othello,* Geoffrey told me I wouldn't be right for Iago, the false friend.

The night before Paul and Shirley left Durrington we had the usual booze-up at the Builders' Arms. All faux bonhomie and "lots of luck, darlings," and the air crackling with disguised jealousy.

I knew one person who was delighted though, and that was Sarah Barnes. She was giving a good performance of looking regretful at losing her leading man, but I knew her well enough to pick out the performance from the truth.

"It won't be the same without Paul," she said to Shirley, and that was true, too.

She was sitting on the bar stool with her long legs folded back. I liked Sarah. I liked her professionalism, and I knew she was good because she never fooled herself, and she didn't need an ego booster like Paul. She fought back her own failures and disappointments. She'd be a great actress some day.

"We shall miss our Paul, won't we, Charlie?" Sarah said to me.

There was a hint of malicious amusement in her black eyes.

"I shall miss you all," Shirley said, but she was looking at me. I wasn't going to tell her that I was packing Durrington in, too, and following them to London. It didn't seem the right moment. Apart from the fact that I'd had Rep, and Rep had had me, I wasn't letting my quarry out of sight.

The next morning, I kissed Shirley on the lips on Durrington station just before the train went out. Her lips were as soft as I remembered them.

"I'm sorry we're leaving, in one way. Perhaps we shall meet again, soon," she said, almost wistfully.

She was standing at the carriage window. Paul was sitting in the opposite corner of the carriage with his feet up on the seat. He waved me a perfunctory goodbye. He was

45

already in London. He was not one to let the last links snap slowly.

"Perhaps," I said. "You never know."

I already had my ticket to London in my pocket. It was valid for three months. Its possession had given me courage for the parting from Shirley.

5

Naturally I didn't remember all this, between questions, at that Scotland Yard interrogation. I sat, sometimes flushed in the face and perspiring, sometimes clammy and pale, knowing they didn't believe I had a chill, and knowing how both of them interpreted the symptoms.

It is a frightening thing to know that accidental physical symptoms, over which you have no control, are leading you to disaster. I know of none worse, for the more you fight against them the more forcefully they surge over you. Like blushing, when you're a kid.

I watched the Inspector turning over some typed pages in his folder. The cat-faced Sergeant was still watching me in an interested sort of way, tapping the table with his government-issue pencil. As if to fill in a gap in the interrogation, he said, "Sure you've nothing to add or amend in that statement?"

"I've told you—nothing at all," I said drearily.

"Well, that's all right then, isn't it?"

I nodded, though I knew that it wasn't all right, I knew that something was going to surface. The Inspector sighed, as though the frailties of human nature were at times too much for him to bear. He said, "We've had a few words here and there with members of this Mr. Paul King's colleagues in Durrington, sir. It seems he wasn't very popular, sir."

"He had talent," I lied. "Talent makes people jealous."

The Inspector nodded, and smiled at the Sergeant. The Inspector said, "Mr. Maither's a very unusual gentleman, Sergeant."

"Exceptional, you could say he was exceptional, sir."

They smiled at each other, knowingly.

"Meaning what?" I asked sharply, and felt the fever flush mounting to my face again. That's the trouble, if you're feverish, the slightest thing sparks off a reaction. "Meaning what, what are you getting at? Go on, what are you getting at?"

The Sergeant put on a phoney surprised look, all wide-eyed and innocent, and sat back in his chair and said in a reproachful tone, "You don't want to get ratty, sir. You don't want to snap the Inspector's head off like that. He was paying you a compliment, the Inspector was, he said you were unusual."

"Christian. I meant you were a very Christian gentleman," the Inspector explained, and from his voice anybody under the age of two would have thought he was deeply hurt.

"It means you're forgiving," he added. "Bearing no grudge."

"Not even when somebody pinches your girl," explained the Sergeant. "This Shirley Baker, she was your girl, wasn't she, sir, till Mr. King came along and married her?"

I hesitated, seeing the path they were beating out ahead, yet unable to avoid it. Everybody at Durrington had known how I felt about Shirley.

"I was very fond of Miss Baker at one time," I said at length, with a sort of ghastly primness which would have deceived nobody, let alone a couple of cops.

"You were in love with her?" the Sergeant asked. "You wanted to marry her?"

"Yes," I said reluctantly, and wiped my forehead again, because the fever was coming out properly now. "Yes, I'd have married her."

"You didn't mention that in your statement, sir."

"You didn't bloody well ask me," I said irritably. "If you'd asked me, it would have saved you sniffing around former members of the cast. It would have saved a lot of time and tax-payers' money, wouldn't it? Well, wouldn't it?"

The Inspector hadn't smoked at all, but now he pulled out a short, stubby pipe and an old-fashioned rubber tobacco pouch. There was a lull while he began to fill it. Then he said, coldly, "There was no occasion to pursue that line of inquiry until we received certain information on the subject. I am pursuing it now, and I propose to pursue it further."

Hitherto, the interrogation had been informal, a crude give and take. Now his precise, metallic remarks increased my fears. What was the source of his information? Once again I had a mental picture of Maynard, the psychiatrist, the refugee who had made good, being questioned by the police. Once again I did him an injustice.

I watched the Inspector take a sheet of typed paper from his folder, at the same time whipping on his spectacles to read it. I had thought of him as a tired automaton, gray-haired, gray-faced, looking forward only to his pension, assured of his material needs, while the Sergeant was the hunter. I saw I was wrong. Both were hunters, only their methods were different.

He looked at me and said, "I quote from a signed statement from a former member of the Durrington Repertory Company. 'Mr. Charles Maither was an actor who should never have entered the profession. Apart from a reasonable diction, he had no other assets. In my opinion he had a chip on his shoulder, which showed itself in his cynical attitude towards the acting profession. He was not without wit, but it was of a cheap, malicious, destructive nature, due to his lack of success. There is no doubt in my mind that he was professionally jealous of Mr. Paul King. It was well known in the company that he was enamored of Miss Shirley Baker, and that her marriage to Mr. King was a grave blow to him. I do not think that he was in any way friendlily disposed to Mr. King. My own relations with Mr. Maither were always friendly.' "

He put the statement back into the folder. I didn't ask who had signed it, because I didn't need to, because only

Geoffrey Glover could have had the insight to produce an analysis like that.

Looking back now, as I record my return visit to Durrington, I remember how I remembered Durrington, and I remember how I tried to remember it during the interrogation. Onion skins of memories, layer upon layer. And in all the layers, until the last layer, there was no sense of guilt about the actual killing of Paul King.

But I remember too, with a feeling of sadness, little diminished by time, the stab to the heart in Geoffrey's statement. The fact that I myself had come to the same conclusion, that I was not fitted for the stage, makes no difference.

I was lighting a third cigarette as the Inspector read from another statement. I heard his voice, unemotional and devoid of tone, droning remorselessly on. " 'It was well known in the cast that there was no love lost between Mr. Maither and Paul King. Most of us thought that Shirley Baker was Charles Maither's mistress, before Paul King came on the scene.' "

"It's a lie," I said loudly. "She never was my mistress."

The Inspector tossed the statement back into the folder and said, "Are you suggesting that it is a false statement?"

"Certainly I am. She never was my mistress."

He looked at the Sergeant, shaking his head, and said, "Funny how they get things wrong, isn't it?"

"Sort of fly off the handle," the Sergeant said. "Even when they're not flustered."

"It's a lie," I said again, hotly. "She never was my mistress!"

"Look, sir," the Inspector said patiently, as though he was talking to a subnormal child, "the statement did not say Miss Baker was your mistress—it said that that was the general impression in the cast, see?"

"What people *thought*," explained the Sergeant. "That's different, isn't it? You in a position to tell what people thought?"

When I said nothing, he asked again, "You in a position to tell what people thought?"

"Skip it," I replied irritably.

The Inspector laughed and said, "Skip it, indeed! It's a serious matter to say somebody has signed a false statement. You can't just shrug it off and say 'skip it,' sir."

"All right, I spoke hastily," I said sourly.

"You wish to retract your remark and admit it is not a false statement, right?"

"If you like," I muttered and heard the Sergeant sigh.

He said, "The Inspector here, he doesn't mind one way or another, see? He just wants to know if you retract or you don't."

"I retract," I said sullenly.

The Inspector got up and walked to the window and stared out at the gray sky, hands in trouser pockets. The Sergeant had begun to draw doodles on a page of his notebook.

The Inspector said, without turning round, "The lady who made this statement, why did she say it was generally known in the cast that there was no love lost between you and Mr. Paul King?"

"How do I know why she said it? She was wrong."

"And everybody else who thought it was wrong?"

I couldn't be sure, but I guessed that the "she" who had made the statement was gawky Sarah Barnes.

The Inspector said, "And everybody else who thought it was wrong?"

I nodded, and said, "He wasn't popular. Whoever made that statement just lumped me in with the rest. There was no love lost between Paul King and *any* member of the cast."

"Except his wife, Shirley, I suppose?" said the Sergeant, still doodling, not looking up. "And you. He pinched your girl friend and married her, but he remained your close friend. Very forgiving, very Christian, sir. Pity there aren't more people like you around."

"Very forgiving, genuine Christian attitude," agreed the Inspector, and turned and came back to the table and sat down heavily.

"I got him his job with Reg Taylor, the London manager," I said suddenly, triumphantly. "I got him his first real chance."

"Because he was your friend?"

"And a good actor," I said, though the words nearly stuck in my throat. "He deserved a chance, Paul did."

The Inspector put his hands, palm downwards, on the table, and leaned towards me, chin thrust forward, black eyebrows drawn together. I was beginning to know this attitude and braced myself.

"Why?" he asked sharply, "why was he your close friend? If the rest of the cast disliked him, why was this man, who had stolen your girl, a close friend? Why the bloody hell should you be the one who was his friend? Why did you get him his first chance, go on, tell us why?"

"I've told you," I replied uneasily, "he was a good actor. And I thought he was more sinned against than sinning."

"The bond of friendship wouldn't have been his wife? Putting up with Paul King, so that you could hang around his wife? Currying favor with his wife by getting him a job with this Mr. Taylor, hoofing off to London, directly Paul King ended up there? There's some might think you were still in love with her."

"Lusting after her," said the Sergeant primly. "Hanging around, waiting your chance, that's what some might think."

"Actors are catty," I said, trying to sound scornful. "You want to take what they say with a grain of salt."

"We do," said the Inspector, heartily.

"We do, indeed," said the Sergeant, and stared at me with his catlike hunter's look.

"But we come against difficulties," the Inspector said. "Like people who aren't actors."

"Like statements from people who aren't actors," the Sergeant said, and looked at the Inspector and smirked.

The Inspector went harking back to grains of salt. So did the Sergeant. I began to wish I had never mentioned grains of salt.

The Inspector said, "Certainly we take what actors say with a grain of salt."

"Do you know," said the Sergeant earnestly, "we'd even take what *ex*-actors say with a grain of salt. Funny, isn't it?"

"Meaning me?" I asked defiantly.

"Nobody mentioned you, sir," the Inspector said, in a phoney astonished tone of voice. He looked at the Sergeant, leaning back in his chair, black eyebrows raised. He said to the Sergeant, "I never mentioned grains of salt in connection with Mr. Maither, did I, Sergeant?"

"Not in my hearing, sir," said the Sergeant. "Mr. Maither, here, he mentioned salt, sir, not you."

The sweat was beginning to form on my forehead again, and I felt the fever-driven blood rising to my cheeks. I didn't bother to get out my handkerchief, I just wiped my brow with the back of my hand, and said, "Oh, for God's sake, forget about grains of salt!"

The Sergeant looked up at the Inspector, smiled slightly, and looked down at his notebook again and murmured, "One moment these people are keen on salt, and the next they aren't, sir. One moment they are talking about taking grains of salt, and the next they are telling you to forget salt. That's human nature, I suppose."

The Inspector ignored him. He was staring at me, thoughtfully, and I thought he was maneuvering to a new starting line. But he wasn't. He double-tracked back to non-actors. Normally, he spoke in a quiet tone, now he said, suddenly and harshly, "I'll take what actors said with one of these grains of salt you mentioned—but what about people who are trained to record things? What about a non-actor who has signed a statement that during the time you were at Durrington you said the death of Mr. Paul King would be a good thing?"

"Nasty, unkind thing to say about a close personal friend," the Sergeant said, softly.

"I never said anything of the sort," I said indignantly.

The Inspector glanced at a typed statement, then looked up.

"This witness states that you had some farfetched plan of breaking the marriage by promoting Mr. King's career. He is a man trained to record and remember things accurately."

I looked at him puzzled and bewildered, not getting his line of thought.

"Record things?"

"Report things," the Sergeant said. "Report things accurately."

"Like reporters," the Inspector explained.

"Newspaper reporters," the Sergeant said patiently. Now I knew the slip I had made in Durrington.

They had gone, Paul and Shirley, and with them had temporarily gone the stress and the strain, the burden of seeming a friend to Paul King, when inwardly I hated him and wished him ill. For a short while the load was lifted. I still had to bear it in the presence of the cast during the weeks I remained at Durrington. But for half an hour or so, after Paul and Shirley's train had drawn out of the station, I rejoiced in my freedom.

For a few seconds, I had let my guard down.

Now, gazing over the Inspector's shoulders at the drifting gray clouds, I knew I was faced with the consequences of a few seconds' incautious emotion. The fever flush surged back into my face.

"Feeling flustered?" asked the Sergeant.

"I've got a chill," I muttered and wiped my brow again.

6

I remembered how Paul King came to the carriage window just before the train left. A cameraman from the *Durrington News* took a picture of him and Shirley looking out of the window, waving graciously to the non-existent crowd. There had also been Jim Withers, a reporter, to catch his dramatic parting message—how happy he had been in Durrington, which he hadn't, and how he hoped that maybe one day he would come back and play in the theatre again, which was the last thing he wanted, of course—meanwhile he was eagerly looking forward to the challenge of the future, and all that baloney. Local Boy About to Make Good stuff. Okay for a single-column picture and a couple of paragraphs, the latter mostly about Reg Taylor, who'd probably fixed it with the editor, anyway.

I watched the train draw out then walked along the station and into the Railway Arms for a pint of beer to cheer myself up. Jim Withers, the reporter, had had a similar idea, except that he was drinking whisky.

He nodded to me as I came in. He was a thin middle-aged chap with a white face, the skin stretched tightly over the bone structure. He had false teeth which made him sound as though he had a pebble in his mouth when he talked, and he wore spectacles with a dark frame. He had cold, merciless eyes, colored like those of a goat, and was one of those cautious, withdrawn characters who never say anything openly and hint darkly that they know more than they do.

"Well, that's our Paul," I said. "Off on the high road to success—if I may coin a phrase."

Withers looked at me with his emotionless eyes. I had the feeling that nobody need lack an enemy who had Jim Withers for a friend.

"Good riddance," he said.

"Why? Did you know him?"

"I didn't know him. I never said I did, did I? I said, I never said I did, did I?"

"No, well, I just wondered why—"

"I never said I *knew* him—not personally, I didn't. I said, not *personally*, I didn't."

He fixed me with his unblinking, yellowish goat's eyes, saying nothing, going into one of his silent, enigmatic moods.

"Look," I said, "I only wondered—"

"Yes, well, that's all right, then, isn't it?"

I nodded and gave it up. He was one of those people who somehow always make you think you've accused them of something.

Suddenly he added, "But then, I never knew Napoleon

Bonaparte, did I? I said, I never knew Bonaparte, did I? But I know a lot about him. See what I mean?"

I nodded again and said nothing. I wasn't interested in all this guff.

"He was born in Accringham, see?"

"Was he?" I said, out of politeness, because Accringham was another town like Durrington, dead dull, and industrial.

Withers said, "My brother, he worked in Accringham."

I was staring at my beer as he said it, and I went on staring at it, though somewhere at the back of my mind I heard the old vibrant tinkling, like those kitchen ping-ers which tell you when the cabbage is ready cooked.

I heard him say, "His name isn't Paul King, see? It's John Moore."

The tinkling became less vibrant, in fact it died away in a desultory anticlimax, as I said, "A lot of actors adopt other names."

"John Moore, son of Harry Moore."

He looked at me again with his infuriating significant gaze, as if he, Jim Withers, was the confidant of Cabinet Ministers and had just let fall a valuable government secret.

"So what?" I asked irritably.

He shrugged and ordered another whisky for himself.

"Oh, forget it. Don't worry about it; I said don't worry about it, see, forget it."

"Okay," I agreed, "if that's what you want."

But naturally it wasn't at all what he wanted. I watched him pay for his whisky, picking up the change, coin by coin, looking at each one with his cold eyes as though there might be a forgery among them.

"My brother, Pete, Inspector in the Accringham police," Withers said. "See what I mean?"

The ping-er was going again, but unenthusiastically. My interest was aroused, of course, but after the anticlimax about the changes of names, I wasn't expecting too much. Perhaps a matter of a dud check or a bottle of after-shave lotion nicked from a supermarket.

"Go on," I said briefly. I couldn't be bothered to cajole him any more.

"My brother Pete was over here a week or two ago. Stayed the night. We went to the Rep and afterwards he said, Paul King, recognize him, he said, he's John Moore, he said. Described six years ago as an unemployed actor at a coroner's court in Accringham."

"Coroner's court?"

"His girl friend, lass called Beryl Wilson, hanged herself because he'd chucked her up. That's what the coroner decided. She was only a kid of nineteen."

"Ah," I said, and left it at that. But after a while, when he said nothing, I added, "Paul King give evidence?"

"John Moore gave evidence. Paul King—John Moore— he stood in the coroner's court, looking fair haired and bewildered, kind of forlorn and lost, that's how brother Pete described him. Cast-iron evidence, see? Letter from him to her breaking it off. Letter from her to him, say she couldn't live without him, he was her whole life. Coroner said it was a sad case, but kids of that age were entitled to change their minds before it was too late. My brother Pete was a sergeant at the time. Seeing Paul King last week brought it back to him. We got on well together, Pete and I. He told me things. See what I mean? I said, he told me things."

He had reverted to being cryptic and mysterious again.

"What things?" I said obediently.

"Things."

"Ah," I said, as though I understood, which I didn't.

"Like how many women commit suicide by hanging themselves. See what I mean?"

"Not exactly."

Withers looked at me pityingly and shrugged, and said, "Let's forget it, shall we?"

But when I said nothing, and just stared at my beer, he added, "Practically none—these days. Mostly do it with sleeping pills. Sometimes gas. See what I mean?"

I was getting the implication now all right, and was pretty shaken. Much as I disliked Paul King, I thought that to imply that he murdered the girl Beryl Wilson was outlandish, farfetched and, of course, a criminal slander.

"You can't base murder suspicions on suicide statistics," I muttered. "Anyway, there were the letters."

That sparked him off all right. He swung round, staring at me with his cold goat's eyes behind the black frames, pale face taut beneath the white skin.

"I didn't say anything about murder; I said I didn't say anything about murder, did I?"

"Well, not actually," I replied quickly.

"Either I did, or I didn't. I said, either I did, or I didn't—well, did I?"

"No."

"Well, then? You want to be careful not put words into people's mouths, you know. It can lead to trouble, it bloody can. I tell you that. I said, I tell you that—straight."

He finished his whisky, said he must get back to the office, turned to go, then stopped and said, "As for the letters—my brother Pete, he had to make the report on the case. He told me the letter from this chap King had lots of fingerprints on it. King's of course, and the people who owned the house—they were away for the night, when she did it, see?—and the police constable who found her, and his own, Pete's see? But not hers, not the deceased, so to speak. Not such as to be recognized. Lots of smudges here and there, see? Nothing that could be described as hers. And no envelope."

"No envelope?" I said feebly. "No bloody envelope?"

"No bloody envelope. 'Course she might have torn it up, maybe that's what she did," he added sarcastically. "Tore it up. Then displayed the letter so that all could see it."

I said nothing. I wouldn't say I was listening to the turmoil of thoughts in my head, because there wasn't much to listen to, unless you can say you are listening to a noisy fog. But in the end, I said, "Did your brother point this out to people—to his Inspector?"

"'Course he did."

"And?"

"And nothing. He hadn't got any influence, see, not in those days. They wouldn't even let him send the rope to the laboratory. Open and shut case, they said. Letters proved it."

"They didn't prove it," I muttered. "They didn't *prove* anything."

Withers felt in his pocket for some cigarettes. He said, "They didn't *disprove* it, did they?"

"What about the rope?" I said. I wasn't interested in the rope, I just wanted to keep him talking, about the letters, about the rope, about anything.

"What about it, what about the rope?" I repeated.

"Just a rope—except the people in the house had never seen it before. Funny, eh? Spontaneous suicide by a young girl with a rope she happened to find handy which the house owners had never seen before. Just a bit she happened to find about her. Often happens, doesn't it," he added acidly. "I'm not suggesting anything, see? Got that clear? I'm not suggesting anything. Nothing, not bloody likely, I'm not."

I looked towards the bar, put a hand under his elbow, said, "Yes, you are. Why?"

He ignored the question. He said, "It'll have to be a quick one."

I ordered whiskies for both of us, and said again, "What about the rope—what about it?"

"Nothing about it. They didn't examine it in the lab. He hadn't any influence in those days, Brother Pete hadn't."

"And if they had examined it?" I muttered. "What if they had?"

He looked at me, hostile, suspicious, yet tempted to talk.

"Probably nothing. Too many people had handled it. Not evidence to produce in court."

He took a sip of whisky, and I did likewise, and said, "Jim?"

"What?"

"You might as well come clean. What's on your mind, what was on your brother's mind?"

Suddenly his resistance seemed to collapse. It was a few

minutes before I knew why. He still spoke abruptly, but it was as though he had made a psychological jump.

"Brother Pete used a magnifying glass, and the hairlike rope fibers were pointing the wrong way, see?"

He saw I didn't see, had no reason to see, couldn't be expected to see. I was looking at him as before, bemused, still trying to grope my way through the fog which now was noisy with staggering and terrible thoughts.

I heard him say, "She had a room at the top of the house. There was a beam. She had apparently thrown the rope over the beam, and eventually kicked away the chair beneath her. So that was that," he said, and shrugged.

"Except?"

"The hairlike rope fibers pointing the wrong way. But not enough of them. Too many people had handled the rope — and too carelessly."

He paused, then looked round almost conspiratorially, then said, "It's like this, Brother Pete says—if it's genuine suicide, some of the fibers will be pointing *away* from the noose, where the rope passed over the beam, on the downward drop, see? If — if the person was killed first, then hauled up to simulate suicide, the hair fibers will be pointing the other way, that's what Brother Pete said. Now do you see? I said, now do you see?"

I nodded, saying nothing for a moment, thinking: no envelope, therefore no postmark, no discernible fingerprints of the girl on the letter, the rope fibers, the preference of women for suicide by barbiturates rather than other methods.

"There was Harry Moore," Withers said.

"What about Harry Moore?"

"His father."

"I know about that. A drunk. Left his wife while Paul was a kid. Disturbed family background for a child."

He looked at me again, a bitter, sneering expression on his lips but not in his eyes. No expression in his eyes.

"It could have been more disturbed. I said, it could have been more disturbed."

"I wouldn't know," I said irritably.

"You wouldn't know? Well, I would, see? Five years after he left his wife, Harry Moore was committed to a mental asylum. And five years later he died there. Bad blood, that's what Paul King's got—I said bad blood. That's why I said good riddance."

The months of emotional repression suddenly built up inside me. The Railway Arms had two doors and from the outside one I heard the rumble of traffic on the streets, and from the other, which was at the end of a station platform, I heard a whistle and the sound of another train pulling out. But I heard no urgent warning bell to make me guard my tongue. Paul King had left Durrington, and I, too, would soon be gone. The years ahead were blank pages, the fatal end of the story unknown and unpredictable. I looked into the cold, repellent eyes of Jim Withers and almost liked him.

"Paul King is a ruthless, self-centered bastard," I said vehemently. "If he dropped dead tomorrow it would be no loss to the world in general or the theatre in particular. And he's probably got sadistic tendencies."

"I'm sorry for his wife," said Jim Withers, "I said, I'm sorry for his wife. Soft little thing. Too good for that heel, but she'll never leave him. They never do; I said, they never do."

Good old goat's-eyes, I thought, what with the beer and the whisky and the relaxation of tension, good old goat's-eyes, we're on the same beam about Paul, goat's-eyes and I, in the Railway Arms, and I heard myself saying, "I'll bust his marriage. I'll make him a star, see? I've got him his first chance already."

"You mad?" he asked. "You gone barmy, or something?"

"You just see," I said viciously, "you bloody well see. She won't leave *him,* but he'll leave *her.* The rocket sheds its booster, the new star sheds his wife. I'll bust his bloody marriage, that's what I'll do. I'll bust his marriage."

I stopped, aware that Jim Withers was looking at me with as much surprise as his stony nature would allow him to show. Even I was astonished at the venom which I had allowed to creep into my voice.

"Tell Brother Pete to put that bit about sadistic tendencies into his dossier," I added more evenly.

"What dossier?" Withers said scornfully. "The case is stone-cold dead. You don't know much about the police, do you? You don't think they keep a case open all these years after a coroner's verdict like that, do you?"

"He can tuck it away in the back of his head," I said indifferently.

Withers swallowed the remains of his whisky and turned to go, and this time he did go, only before he went he passed his hand lightly over the lower part of his body.

Then he said, "Brother Pete hasn't got a back of the head."

I smiled politely, thinking he was being funny, that he was playing down his brother's memory capacity, but he said in his hard, metallic voice, "Brother Pete was killed on the way back home last week—run into by a lorry. Head on crash. Lorry's steering failed. It was in the newspapers," he added, almost accusingly.

Like many actors, I mostly read the theatre and general entertainment news. All I could say, lamely, was that I was sorry.

He shrugged and said, "If it isn't one way it's another."

He was looking at me in an uncharacteristic way, not hostilely or challengingly, or with his usual implied resentment of the world, but calmly, like a man who has come to a difficult decision and was glad to be shot of the burden of worry.

He said, "You're the only one who knows Brother Pete's ideas. You're in the same profession as Paul King. Might help if there's a murder within ten thousand miles of Paul King, or a suicide which might have been faked. Keep an eye on his wife," he added almost gently.

A feeling of helplessness made me hold out my hands to him, over dramatically, perhaps, as an actor might, and ask him loudly, "How the hell can I keep an eye on Shirley—share their bedroom or something?"

He listened to my outburst, looking at me distastefully, then said, "I didn't say you could protect her, did I? But you might avenge her. If he's done it once, he could do it again—in a different way, of course."

I was too appalled to say much. All I could say was, "I'd need your backing before the police would take any notice."

I saw his hand pass lightly over his stomach again.

"I don't think I'll be around," he said, coldly.

"Why? Are you ill? What's the matter?"

Instantly he reverted to his old manner, stared at me with hostile goat's eyes, and said, "That's my bloody business, isn't it? I said that's my business, isn't it?"

Thus he spoke and walked away. I never saw him again to speak to.

7

So I knew who had sparked off the police inquiries among the former members of the cast. I could imagine him staring with his yellowish eyes at a sheet of paper and typing his letter about me to Scotland Yard. I expect he relished doing it.

"I'd have thought Jim Withers was dead," I said shakily.

"Well, he isn't, is he?" the Inspector said. "He was very much alive when I saw him. You remember the conversation, then?"

"Did he tell you that Paul King may have caused his earlier girl friend's death, up in Accringham? Did he tell you that?" I asked sharply.

"It's a lot of hooey, that," the Inspector said. "It's the bunk, good and proper."

The Inspector's hands were large and strong, the finger tips square, the nails very clean. In his well-pressed dark-gray suit and white shirt, with discreet dark-blue tie, he could have been a benevolent company executive. At home he was probably a kind husband and father. He wasn't at home, and he wasn't my father, and he didn't sound benevolent when he spoke.

He sounded tired and irritated when he said, "This statement you made after Mr. King's death—I take it that you were thinking of the comradely Durrington days when you said that Mr. King was 'a close and personal friend in the provinces and the friendship was maintained, unbroken, when you came to London.'?"

I challenged them, then, knowing it would cause trouble. "I didn't say that at first. I said he was a personal friend. Then you suggested 'close personal friend.'"

The Inspector flung himself back in his chair and said, "That's a serious accusation, sir!"

"Suggesting that the Inspector here put words in your mouth is serious. Very serious," the Sergeant snapped. "That could do him a bit of no good in his career, that could. I'm surprised at you trying to wriggle out of things like that."

"I am not trying to wriggle out of anything!"

"Well, that's all right then, isn't it? You withdraw the remark, and the Inspector here'll overlook it. Right?"

"No," I muttered, "I bloody well don't withdraw it."

"Anybody force you to sign the statement?" the Inspector asked sharply. "Going to say next that I pointed a gun at your head?"

"Or twisted your arm?" the Sergeant said.

"Friend or close personal friend, it didn't seem to matter," I replied impatiently. "I wanted to get shot of the whole thing."

"Shot's an unfortunate word," murmured the Sergeant. "In the circumstances."

"Skip it," murmured the Inspector.

He leaned across the table towards me, tapping the surface with a ballpoint pen. He seemed about to say something, but changed his mind, leaned back again and spoke to the Sergeant.

"There's something daft going on, Sergeant."

The Sergeant laughed, and said, "He comes here today of his own free will—no force—implies he was a bit flustered when he made his statement, agrees he isn't flustered today, re-reads his statement, agrees with it, and now disagrees with it. Maybe he's flustered again, sir?"

"Flusters come and go," the Inspector said. "I've noticed that before with gentlemen like Mr. Maither."

"As and when convenient," the Sergeant said, tapping absent-mindedly on the table with his wooden pencil. They were great tappers, both of them. "One moment a fluster is *not* there, and next moment it *is* there, depending on what statements are taken out of the folders, sir."

"I know what you're getting at," I said, and stopped, searching for convincing words, groping for them through a mist of dismay.

"With respect, that's more than the Inspector can say about you."

"What I want to say is this," I began, but stopped again and shivered slightly because of the chill inside me.

They both said nothing, looking at me, the Inspector stroking the side of his nose, the Sergeant doing his alert feline act. In the end, the Inspector said, "What *do* you want to say, sir?"

"You've got a business to look after," added the Sergeant, looking ostentatiously at his watch. "You said so. The Inspector here's got other work, too."

I took a deep breath. I didn't think I could put it over, but when you are cornered you try anything.

I said, "You can be a friend to somebody without liking him. You can even *help* him without liking him. Can't you? Well, can't you?"

The Inspector sniffed, rubbed his nose. He said, quoting from a typed page, in a droning voice, "'Mr. Maither thought the world in general and the theatre in particular would be well rid of him, if he died.' That's what you allegedly said, sir."

He stared at the ceiling. The Sergeant stared at one end of a fingernail. I shook my head.

"I didn't use those words. Anyway, you can *hate* somebody and still not do him any harm. Can't you? That's true, isn't it?"

The Sergeant looked up from his fingernail and said, "Real Christian attitude?"

"I'm not saying that."

The Inspector sighed.

"Look, we're not deaf, sir. We know you're not saying it, the Sergeant's saying it. 'Real Christian attitude,' that's what he said. Thou shalt love thy neighbor as thyself."

"Thou shalt not covet thy neighbor's wife," added the Sergeant, with one of his prim looks. "Did you covet your neighbor's wife, sir?"

The Inspector leaned forward, hands on table, palms down.

"Don't reply if you feel flustered. That's all we ask—just don't reply if you feel flustered. The Sergeant and I, we don't want any more of the flustered stuff. Get a legal adviser, if you want one, don't reply if you don't want to, but for heaven's sake don't give us any more of the flustered stuff. Can we take it you were in love with Mr. King's wife, and that you hated him?"

"Or are all these signed statements a lot of balderdash?" asked the Sergeant.

The human spirit reacts strangely. Most of the time it is influenced by the instinct of survival. In difficulties it twists and turns, wriggles and deceives, but suddenly it reacts unexpectedly, perhaps to an amalgam of self-respect, loyalty to an ideal, loyalty to an individual, and sheer exasperation.

"I loved Shirley as far back as the Durrington days," I said defiantly. "There's nothing in the statement I signed after Paul King's death to say I didn't love her."

A lawyer, of course, would never have let me say it. He'd have interrupted, banged the table, objected loudly to the question, done anything to shut me up while he glared at me or kicked me under the table. But there wasn't a lawyer, and I hadn't wanted a lawyer, and I said it.

"Nobody said there was," said the Sergeant cheerfully. "Nobody said that at all. The Inspector never suggested that."

"Nor did the Sergeant," added the Inspector. "It just helps to know it. Clears the air a bit, gets rid of some of the fog. And getting back to this Christian attitude, you agree you weren't heartbroken by this unfortunate gentleman's death? In your signed statement, you said—"

But I interrupted him. I said heatedly, "I didn't say in my signed statement that I was heartbroken. I said I was *shocked.*"

"He was shocked," murmured the Sergeant. The Inspector nodded, thought for a moment and agreed.

"He was shocked. He thought the world in general, and he and the theatre in particular, were well rid of Mr. King, but—"

I banged the table and said loudly, "In view of what Jim Withers' brother said and my own personal feelings, how could I be heartbroken?"

They didn't expect this outburst. They looked at me in silence for a few seconds.

The Sergeant said mildly, "You don't want to get angry with the Inspector, sir. It doesn't help."

"I wasn't being angry," I said bleakly, "I was being emphatic."

"He was being emphatic," murmured the Inspector soothingly.

The Sergeant had been scribbling shorthand in his notebook from time to time. He looked at the Inspector, and said quietly, "He'll probably want to make another statement amending the one he made after Mr. King's death, sir."

"Later," murmured the Inspector, "he may want to later."

"If he can spare the time from his business," said the Sergeant, and turned his head to watch my expression. He disliked me personally. The feeling was mutual.

The Inspector stroked the side of his nose for a second or two. I noted he had dark shadows under his eyes. He was overworked all right. I might have been sorry for him at any other time.

I tried to go off on another tack. I said, "The story which Jim Withers told me, the facts he had got from his brother—"

The Inspector broke in quickly.

"Never mind Jim Withers, never mind his brother, not at the moment."

66

"I do mind," I protested. The Sergeant said, "I bet you do."

I felt myself losing my temper.

"Stop mucking me about! I'm fed up with it."

I saw a gleam appear in his cold blue eyes. If he'd had long whiskers they would have been twitching, if he'd had a tail it would have been lashing from side to side.

"Who's mucking who about?" he asked harshly. "Tell me and the Inspector that, sir—who's mucking who about? We're not mucking you about, you don't want to say silly things like that, you don't."

"Not in your position," added the Inspector smoothly.

"What do you mean 'my position'?"

The Sergeant flung his pencil down. He said, "Making a signed statement, saying you were flustered, making accusations against the Inspector here, confirming things, denying things, saying you acted in a Christian way towards this Mr. Paul King."

"When you knew you plotted to bust up his marriage," said the Inspector coldly. "Proper Christian attitude that was. Pretending to be his friend, and plotting to bust his marriage."

"Look, I never introduced this 'Christian attitude' talk, you did!" I said angrily. "So just bloody well stop it!"

"Keep your temper," said the Inspector.

"Pipe down," said the Sergeant.

I looked at the Inspector and said, hopelessly, "Why don't you say what you think?"

"And what am I supposed to be thinking?"

"What's the Inspector supposed to be thinking?" pressed the Sergeant. "Tell Detective Chief Inspector Williams here what he's supposed to be thinking, go on, have a bash, tell him what you think he's thinking."

I swallowed and fumbled for my packet of cigarettes, took out a cigarette and lit it. The flame trembled. I said nothing, staring across the room to the window, watching the gray rain clouds gathering.

"You're thinking I killed Paul King," I said at last, defiantly.

"Wrong," said the Inspector, and gave an artificial laugh.

"You don't want to have pessimistic thoughts like that," said the Sergeant. He spoke with a ghastly cheerfulness, so obviously exaggerated that I could not fail to see it, which was what he intended.

The Inspector said, "I was thinking what signed statement I'd make if I was in your shoes and *accused* of killing this poor Mr. King."

"Which he's not accused of," said the Sergeant, quickly.

The Inspector said, dreamily, "I think I'd say, 'bearing in mind the facts supplied by the reporter, Jim Withers, and having been engaged in a heated argument, I temporarily lost my temper and accused him to his face of having been responsible for a certain young woman's death. He turned very pale and seized an Indian dagger which lay upon the table between us. He attacked me, and I shot him in self defense.' That's what I might say."

"With an automatic pistol which I happened to have about me," murmured the Sergeant, and smiled. "He'd have to do better than that, sir."

"He probably could."

They stopped talking and looked at me, waiting for me to take the lead they'd suggested. I said woodenly, "It wasn't like that. It wasn't like that at all."

They went on staring at me. I felt the fever flush rising again to my cheeks, and the perspiration gathering at the roots of my hair. At other times I might have felt no temptation to give way. But now, having yielded in the matter of my love for Shirley, I suddenly wanted rest, a bed, any bed, even a cell bed.

I began to shiver, conscious of my physical fatigue, almost indifferent to the pit towards which I felt myself sliding provided only that there was a bed of some sort in it. I heard myself say, almost casually, "We did, in fact, have a difference of opinion about money at our last meeting."

Part Two
In Orbit

8

So we parted for a few months, on Durrington station, Paul and Shirley and I.

A lot can happen in a few months but a lot didn't happen. All that happened was that Paul's play folded, went up in smoke at the theatre at Golder's Green, where there's also a crematorium, and Paul was out on his ear. Right in the cold.

They were living in a room in Earls Court. Savings soon go. Paul was spending part of his time helping out in a coffee bar. Shirley was doing odd jobs on radio, because of her sweet voice.

I didn't see much of them. I had no excuse to. Also I had to try to earn a living. I wasn't having any breaks, either. Writing fifty letters to managements, big and small, and not getting a sausage in reply makes you ponder about the future.

One morning, I decided to hang around the Salisbury public house, where theatre people go, in St. Martin's Lane, making half-a-pint last out. You never know, you could sometimes pick up the trail of a job in such places. The coat-of-arms over the pub door amuses me. It is lozenges with a

number of little lions, quartered (if that's the right heral-
dic phrase) with yellow crocodiles. It has been described
as a load of small stars with two theatrical managers ramp-
ant. I looked at the crocodile managers. They had long
teeth. Type cast. I went into the pub.

I couldn't see anyone I knew. There were girls in head-
scarves and a beautiful, aging queer with a black polo-
necked sweater and a gold medal and a golden cardigan to
match his golden hair. Quite sweet, really, if you like that
sort of thing.

A Yank beside me said to his boy friend, "We must keep
the front boys happy."

"I do so agree, Al."

He probably had to, or he might have been stuck with
paying for the drinks.

"The script is marvelous, marvelously witty—with Queen
Victoria throwing the music stand at Prince Albert, and
Prince Albert throwing the metronome back. Could be it's
above the heads of the public."

It sounded subtle.

"I must dash," said the Yank. "By the way, Bud said to
tell you all the best."

"Thanks, Al, be seeing you."

"Real soon," said the Yank, without conviction.

The girl next to me at the counter was tricked out like
a Woolworth edition of Elizabeth Taylor. Her heapy make-
up looked unappetizing close to the cheese sandwiches.
She was making a cup of coffee last, same as I was the beer.

Then, just before I could duck out, I saw Bob Grange.
He was about forty, used to be quite attractive to women.
If he'd been born earlier he would have been one of those
"laddie boy" actors who were around in the 'twenties.

"Hello, Charlie," he said.

I liked old Bob but he needn't imagine I was going to stake
him a pint, I thought, but when I told him I was "out," he
bought me a pint instead. And he gave me two tickets for
the show he was in at Richmond.

"You'll enjoy it, old boy, we're doing *Flare Path.*"

I could see I would have to go. No good pretending I was too busy. Not when I couldn't buy him a pint back.

"I've given you seats for Friday," said old Bob, "it's usually a good house on Friday."

Bit odd, him having those tickets in his pocket, I thought, but when I brooded about it, it wasn't odd at all. Who would want to go all the way out to Richmond to see old Bob playing *Flare Path* in February?

"I got a few comps," said Bob. "I've just been seeing Francis Maxwell. He may be coming down on Friday. We've got a terrible actor playing the lead. By contrast, I ought to show up well in the Polish officer part."

But he was wrong about that. Flu strikes in February, and it struck the leading man, and when I opened my program, a slip fell out. I saw Paul's name on it. He was understudy, he was playing the young British Air Force officer. Giving the same performance I knew so well. Sympathetic and wanting the audience to love him, which they did. Poor old Bob hadn't a chance, if I knew anything. Not if I could help it, either.

After the show, I went round, and bumped into Paul, slap into him in the corridor. He looked thinner these days, and more like a poor student than ever.

I greeted him. Over heartily, I thought, but still, you can't always judge your performance, not when it's unrehearsed.

"I thought you were tremendous," I said, because it's the sort of thing you say.

He gave me that detached look I knew so well.

"Nice of you to come round, Charlie," he said, absently. I gave him my sympathetic, good old Charlie smile.

"Did you know Francis Maxwell was in front?" I asked innocently. His expression changed immediately. "Bob sent him tickets."

It's not every day a West End producer takes an interest in a local production when the understudy is playing the lead. I don't often feel such a heel as I felt then, doing the dirt on poor old Bob Grange. But you have to keep your aim in view. I had been feeling pretty low, too. Latterly the idea of helping Paul to reach fame and then ditch Shirley had seemed laughable. The way things had been going, it was a question, not of stardom, but of who would first be queueing up for National Assistance.

So I ditched old Bob.

I knew my Paul. He wasn't one to let a drifting lifebelt float by to another man.

"I'll just pop down to the stage door to see if there are any letters for me," he said.

He disappeared round the angle of the corridor and I went on into Bob's dressing room. Bob was taking off his make-up.

"Did you see Francis Maxwell at the stage door?"

"No."

"I told you I sent him a couple of tickets."

He might as well have given them to a barmaid at the Salisbury.

That was how it happened that for the second time I saw Shirley alone while Paul was chatting up a producer. As soon as she opened the door I knew why I hadn't heard her lately on the radio. She didn't look well, and she was pregnant. I put my arms round her and kissed her on both cheeks.

"I *am* so glad to see you," she said.

"I should have come before, but—"

"I wish you had," she said, quickly.

There was a fervent note in her voice. I could hear she felt she needed me. Her hair was untidy, her skirt was crooked and she had done up her blouse with a safety pin. She wasn't wearing her glasses and had peered at me myopically for a split second before she recognized me. I loved her more than ever, the soppy old date, but don't ask me why.

We went into the sitting room, which was even barer than the hall. It was one of those so-called "nice large rooms" I knew so well, and the gas fire was only on half, although it was very cold.

"It's so good to see you, Charlie!" she insisted.

For once, she hadn't immediately asked me where Paul was. I could well imagine that Paul hadn't been at his best out of work. Rugged genius unrecognized can be hard to live with.

"How are *you* doing?" she asked. I was sitting beside her on the sagging settee. It was very hard for me not to put my arms round her. I suppose a self-confident, good looking guy might have tried it, but not me.

"I'm not doing," I said. "I think I'm going to chuck the business."

She looked at me seriously. I could see she was thinking about Paul again, wondering whether he should do likewise. Paul, always Paul, always back to Paul, I thought, with a sudden flare of rage against him.

"I was down at the theatre tonight," I said. "Francis Maxwell came round. I think Paul went off for a drink with him."

Instantly, of course, she was all sparkle and optimism, flushed, eyes shining, speculating, excited about what might happen.

"Charlie! How wonderful! How sweet of you to come straight round to tell me."

I smiled, letting her think that was the reason I'd come. You have to take the breaks when they happen, even small ones. Besides, I had Paul's interests at heart. Too true, I did.

We were cooking the supper together when Paul came in. I could see he'd been successful. He was so full of himself, and his own concerns, he didn't notice the happy atmosphere between us. He had even brought a bottle of wine on the strength of Maxwell's promise of a job.

"I'm damned pleased for you!" I said, and patted him on the back. Good old Charlie was being happy at the prospect of a break for his friend. "Maybe the tide has turned!"

"Maybe," he said briefly, suddenly thoughtful.

It could have been my imagination, but I thought his eyes rested resentfully on Shirley's swelling stomach. He wasn't a man who liked to be impeded.

She didn't notice. She was looking at Paul, as if she couldn't quite believe her good luck. That was a laugh. I remembered how she slogged at Durrington teaching him his inflections, hearing him his lines, boosting his ego, and giving him strong doses of that treacle of human kindness which was his staple diet. *Her* good luck! Some people get things wrong in a big way.

I think I hated him more at that moment than I had ever hated him before. I hated him for the chance he was getting. I hated him for his good looks which had got him the chance. I hated him for the quick contemptuous glance he'd given Shirley. And not least, I hated him for the coming child. For a moment I stared at the floor, in case he saw the expression in my eyes.

I know all about kissing goes by favor, and that the breaks will come in the end, and all that crap, but sitting in outer offices, being told you won't do, hanging around pubs, being given the air by agents, and all those brush-offs and small hellos—as Runyon called them—they don't kind of fill the soul with the milk of human kindness.

I'd watched the bastards at work too often. How they reach for the telephone as soon as you come into the office, and go on reading some bit of paper, just to get you down while you're waiting. Anything to give you the feeling you're a bit of dirt. I was almost at breaking point, then I thought, okay, dirt is dirt. But dirt can do dirt. I looked up at Paul, and, hating him, I smiled my good old Charlie smile.

"It's the best news I've heard for years," I said, my voice filled with the true ring of sincerity. I may not look right on stage, but off stage I can still pull a fast one or two.

Supper was quite gay, with me looking at Paul admiringly, asking him about the part, what the prospects were, and so on and so forth. All the usual codswallop. I even gave him a few tips.

"We had a terrible Christmas," said Shirley.

The wine was warming her up, and she was getting giggly and confidential.

"It was so funny, the woman upstairs gave us the remains of her turkey for a stray cat that comes here. We ate it on Boxing Day—the turkey, I mean."

"I'll get the coffee," said Paul. He went out abruptly.

Shirley stopped laughing, and looked after him, and said awkwardly, "He's had a rough time recently."

Always bloody excuses for him. The wine suddenly tasted sour. Anyway, it was cheap muck.

"It wasn't so bad when I was working, but when the baby began I had to pack it in. I've been feeling so ill. You know how it is—people don't want you, if you can't turn up regularly. I worry about Paul," she went on.

There she was wasting her time, because her husband did all the necessary worrying about himself. Paul got the job. He would.

It was a play called *Beginnings* and Paul was playing a young man who couldn't communicate. What Paul personally had to communicate would have filled a small press cuttings book, about himself. I didn't go to the first night, I was waiting at the hospital while Shirley had the baby. I told the bitchy sister in charge I was Shirley's cousin. No other relations around, and the husband up at the theatre working hard for wife and child. It was a touching story.

Shirley looked beautiful lying in bed. The great tenderness of her expression gave me the same pang I had felt the first day I had seen her. I know all about women looking better after childbirth, and that it's due to some glandular thing, but that doesn't interest me. She was beautiful because I loved her, the gentle, untidy, soppy old date. The baby didn't look in the least like Paul.

Just as well.

The notices were good for the play and for Paul. I thought the play was a stumer. One of those pretentious modern plays, all significant pauses, which suited Paul because he could hog the piece. I was glad I wasn't acting with him. It was no surprise to me he got all the notices.

The theatre wasn't full on the second night. I was told that at a rough guess, there wasn't more than about £ 25 in the dress circle. A *succès d'estime,* as they call it. Always the worst kind of success.

I wasn't pleased about that, of course. It looked as though

we might be back on the old tea-and-sympathy racket which was the last thing I wanted.

The following Saturday, I fetched Shirley from the hospital and brought her back to the flat in a taxi. I'd figured on a happy day settling her in with the baby. I was wrong about that. Ten minutes after we got back, Paul's mother, Edith, turned up.

I've said she was a dreary woman. That was giving her the benefit of the doubt. Edith Moore was a tall, thin, white-faced woman who chain smoked. This isn't unusual, but Edith perpetually rolled her own cigarettes with a small machine. If, for a moment, a cigarette was unlit, it had a small tuft of tobacco hanging off the end of it, like a flag at half-mast. Whenever I saw her she seemed to be wearing ash-colored tweeds. Maybe it was protective coloring, and it also saved giving herself a dust down.

Edith had once had a bit of money, but just to cheer herself up she'd lost it in a speculation. Now, she worked in the W.V.S. in some department which rehabilitated unfortunate families. They were even more unfortunate if they got lumbered with Edith.

There was a ring at the bell just as I was getting Shirley a cup of tea, and there she was. Dear old Edith. Talk about a death's head at the lactation. She sat down in the best chair and, while Shirley was putting the baby in its cot, she sounded off.

"I never think it's a good idea actors having children."

"You think they should be sterilized?" I asked. She gave me a dirty look through the cigarette smoke.

"Acting is a very uncertain profession." She was preaching to the converted.

"You in work?"

I shook my head.

"I wonder you don't give it up," she went on happily. "I mean, you haven't done any good so far. Are you drawing the dole?"

No need to say that Edith had been around during the Depression. Not that she had left it behind, it was with her all the time, and she passed the good news on.

"Of course, I said at the time Paul should never have married. He was far too young. A man on his own is free to go where he likes." And where did your own husband go, I felt like asking, and where did he end up? It's all very well saying some people can't help being soured by life. There's no need to ferment the natural vinegar as she did.

"What are you going to do if you give up acting?" she asked.

"I don't know. I may go in on the management side."

"I thought you needed money for that, backing or whatever you call it," she said, happily.

"There are people who draw salaries in management."

"You mean those people who sit in the Box Office?"

Sweet old thing, Edith was. Endearing, really. Shirley came in. She was wearing a white blouse, and she had pinned her hair up. Her face was fresh and rosy, full of happiness, which was asking for trouble. Edith looked at her. "Oh, dear, you do look washed out," she said.

You couldn't win with Edith.

"I'm just tired," said Shirley, easily.

God knows why she took it from Edith. It never paid off. Even Paul had no use for Edith. She bored him stiff, and no one could say she helped to smooth over the edges of what is laughingly called the marriage tie. Edith was a real pill, the kind of pill you take which makes you feel worse before you get better, and you only feel better when she's gone.

Still, she did revive in me the idea of getting a job in management. I had to face the fact that I was probably finished as an actor.

"How's the play going?"

It was Edith again, her eyes narrowed either against her own smoke screen or because she was eagerly expecting the worst.

"Very well," said Shirley. "Weren't the notices splendid?"

Edith's expression remained submerged.

"Didn't think the *Guardian* did it much good," she said.

"The *Guardian* has a comparatively small circulation," I said.

"I always knew Paul would make it," said Shirley, "it was only a question of waiting."

Everything was a question of waiting, I thought, as I watched the eager expression which had done so much to keep him hoping and believing in himself.

"House full?" asked Edith.

"Oh, yes, always," I said.

This seemed to disappoint her. It was worth a good lie to see her expression.

"Paul had any other offers?"

"Nothing so far. His agent doesn't seem to do a thing," said Shirley.

Edith cheered up at this and poured herself out another cup of tea.

"Didn't think much of Paul in the part," she went on. "Not much at all."

"I thought it showed him up to advantage," I said.

"If only Everet would push him," murmured Shirley.

She sounded worried. It's not good staying with an agent who has known you as a flop. To quote old Runyon again, there's no percentage hanging round a broker and an out-of-work actor is a broker all right. I knew that.

I'm afraid he's out today . . . You just missed him, he's had an urgent appointment with Columbia . . . So sorry, he's in conference. . . ."

I knew the general agent line, even if it wasn't Everet's line. You are not only small, you are seen to be small, and you're made to feel small.

"I wish Paul would get a different agent," said Shirley.

Edith sniffed. "What he needs is a different job."

With this encouragement she departed. Whatever else he'd done, I didn't blame Edith's husband for leaving her soon after Paul was born. It was only surprising he had stayed for the conception, let alone the birth. Paul had said his father drank. I believed him. Only someone plastered out of their mind would have cozied up with Edith.

Then I heard Shirley say, "Paul needs a real success now!" I must say, I found this old disc got on my nerves a bit. "He's terribly unsure of himself."

"Maybe he can't believe he's made it."

"He hasn't yet, has he, Charlie?"

"Not quite yet."

"He just wants a chance," she said, "just one piece of real luck."

"I wish Paul all the luck in the world," I said. I watched her smile affectionately.

"You needn't tell me, Charlie, I know you are saying that from the heart!"

She was dead right. I wished him lots of luck, plenty good, solid destructive luck, to blow up his conceit and vanity and ego, bigger and bigger, till at last it exploded and blew up the marriage.

Good old Charlie.

Some people say you should never go back to certain places, but I did, I went back to Durrington, years after, and strolled about the old, sorrow-filled haunts, seeing the ghosts. After I had wandered round to my old digs, I even went into the Builders' Arms for a cheese sandwich and some beer. The current cast, strangers all to me, were still chattering and muttering over the morning's rehearsal just as I and Vic Jones and the others had all done in the past.

I saw how they glanced at me indifferently, which suited me because there was a far corner where Shirley and Paul King used to sit. I sat down in the corner at the little table and once again Shirley's ghost was there, still fresh looking and happy, and Paul, he was there, too, of course. His ghost face had its usual broody and frustrated look. But at least it was not shattered by a .38 revolver bullet. The skin was unbroken, the bone of the forehead unsplintered. And there was no blood upon it.

I had a mental picture of him lying upon the thick piled carpet of his flat, the blood all about him, and though I gulped the beer I could not eat more than a mouthful or two of the cheese sandwich. I felt sick.

Useless to say it was not on the agenda. Murder seldom is.

9

The luck came, and in a curious way, as strokes of luck so often do. Paul had given me a couple of comps. The show was in a fair way to fold in its third week, what with bad weather, the indifferent play, and the fact that no one had heard of Paul. I took along a magazine girl I knew called Freda Newsome. Freda had been picking my brains for some time about the theatre. She went nuts about Paul. I thought she might.

He could look like one of those dream-sequence men on the covers of women's weeklies. She went back and chattered up her editress about him, and also about a nice double-page feature. Freda had been doing a series on new faces, and had temporarily run short of faces.

Paul was just what the girls wanted. As Freda said, it was nice to be able to assure readers that men like that actually did exist.

Durrington seemed a long way away, in distance and time. So did Jim Withers and brother Pete's theory, but as she spoke it came back to me again, and with a touch of the old fear. The first time I had met Paul in London, I had looked at his hands and his eyes with a feeling of horror. The second time, in the theatre and afterwards, I had almost forgotten Jim Withers. Durrington and the north and all that had gone with it, seemed another, different world. But now, suddenly, Freda's words, that it was "nice to be able to assure readers that men like that actually did exist," had a second and sinister significance and I wondered how "nice" she would think it, if she had heard Jim Withers talking.

I heard about Paul's stroke of luck when Shirley invited me over to thank me. Good old friend Charlie, it's wonderful how he likes to do a good turn when he can.

The only jarring note came when Paul said, "I can't possibly be photographed in this place!" He was angry and humiliated that he should be caught in such a dump. He needn't have worried. Freda came down to spy out the land and do the interview. Later, the photographers arrived in a small van. They filled the sitting-room with table lamps and flowers, and popped plastic daffodils in the garden. The place still looked small—but fancy. In the pictures, Shirley looked the way I knew she could look, beautiful, and ethereal, and even tidy for once.

It was a double feature in three colors. Loads of old crap, of course. But if readers want dream sequences, that's what they get. As for Paul's early sufferings, they would have made the toughest matinee audience cry, even in Glasgow.

Odd thing about that sort of sickly bunk, it often comes true. The double feature caught the eye of a TV producer, Paul was interviewed on the box, and that pepped up the takings at the theatre. The play turned the corner. All the Fleet Street women took Paul up. He was featured alternately as the leader of the new wave of intelligence in the theatre, a rep-to-riches-come-up-the-hard-way-actor and even as a clothes peg for the new type of shirt. Just the old baloney sliced in different ways.

The only thing it hadn't yet pepped up sufficiently was Paul's income. This he pointed out when I went round after a matinee, partly to render homage, that little whiff of professional incense he liked to sniff, and partly to prepare the ground for a little ploy I had in mind. He was sitting in front of the mirror, still wearing his make-up.

"How do you think it went?"

"It's much tighter," I said. "Fantastically better."

It seemed the same old stumer to me, and I'd only sat through half the last act.

"It is going better. I can feel it. Of course, it's not a bad little piece." He'd already become patronizing about the play.

I said solemnly, "It wouldn't play the way it does without you." There's nothing like sincere criticism from a good friend. "Had any new offers yet?"

He had stripped off the dirty shirt he wore in the play,

and was washing at the basin. He looked up at me, his face dripping with water. His eyes still had the same troubled expression, and the dripping water added to the effect. Looked as if he were crying over his own miseries.

"Not a bloody nibble. You'd think Everet would have done something, after all this publicity. I can't pay my bills with pictures in women's magazines, and I didn't even get a fee for them. I need someone who will really push me."

I had conceived a plan involving an agent called Tony Banks, and this was the bit I had to handle carefully. Not too heavy handedly, or the fish would get off the hook.

"I know a man—ex-actor—just getting going as an agent. He's looking for new people."

I left the whole idea hanging in the air. I didn't tell him I had already seen Tony, and mentioned his name.

"Do I know him?"

"Don't think so, I met him on tour about five years ago."

"Any good?"

I shrugged my shoulders, and mentioned a couple of fairly okay names the man had on his books. Even from the quick look in Paul's eyes, I could see he was interested.

"What's his name?"

"Tony Banks."

"Anthony Banks—yes, I think I've heard of him."

"He's not bad. Charming, knows lots of people, and they like him. Tony doesn't take too many people."

That interested Paul, too. It was flattering. Subtle stuff.

"He'd push you. If you go to one of the big people, you become a small cog—unless you're on the international star level."

"Too true."

Paul sat down at his mirror again.

"Tell him to ring me."

"He wouldn't like to poach on Everet. You know how funny agents are. Tell you what I'll do—I'll pop round to his office. I'll just mention casually that you're not too happy."

I could see he was hesitating about whether to take the plunge and leave Everet.

"Don't bother," he said doubtfully.

"It's no bother, his office is only in Orange Street." Paul's play was at the Comedy Theatre, nearly next door. "I'll pop in on my way home."

"You on his books?"

"He wouldn't take me." That stroke told, too. "Besides, I'm thinking of giving up the business."

"What are you going to do?"

"Expect I can find a hole somewhere—on the management side, maybe."

He didn't commiserate with me, and I changed the subject quickly to the thing which really interested him, himself.

"Tony's like you," I said, "up-and-coming." He smiled at me.

"Good of you to help, Charlie," he said, perfunctorily.

It was, but in a way I wanted to do Tony a good turn.

"He'll suit you," I murmured.

I did think so. I thought they would suit one another, and the whole thing would suit me. Tony was a success boy, like Paul.

I had known him on and off for some years. Mostly off. I first met him on tour, when I'd been brought in to take over a part from him. It wasn't surprising he was ducking out. The play wasn't doing well, and Tony wasn't one for helping to keep any ship afloat, except his own. He knew instinctively that when a play or a person gets green mold, it's best not to be in close contact in case any of it rubs off. I wasn't so particular.

Long knives are everywhere, and where the money grows thicker, the knives are longer. But it's difficult to back your fancy in the theatre, where people can become hot properties or dead ducks at the flash of a contract. What adds to the difficulties is that the flops can be dear old chums of the successes. This makes social contact fraught with difficulty, if not impossible. Not that long-term philosophy worried Tony. He skimmed along the top of the waves. Tony was a water skier, and you can only water ski in fine weather.

Still, I liked Tony and he amused me. He had that quick happy wit which can keep a party going, and he liked people, he enjoyed people, and he took them at their own valuation, except when their market was slipping and, even then, he could give them an encouraging slap on the back. He never did anything about them, but at least the gesture showed he had a heart of some sort, somewhere.

He was a good deal older than Paul, and had been able to get parts in the last sunset days of the french window drawing-room comedy.

He had an upper-crust manner, though he hadn't the faintest connection with the upper-crust. His friends, charitable as ever in the theatre world, said this manner came from playing a small part in a William Douglas Home play— son of an Earl, or something.

The decline of upper-crust comedy also put Tony on the skids, but unlike most actors he'd saved a bit of money and he knew a good many people, had charm, and was shrewd about contracts. There seemed to be a niche for him. So he put his bit of cash into the agency business.

I had run into him unexpectedly, and he told me he'd taken up flesh-peddling. We gave one another one of those ecstatic "hello-how-are-you-getting-on" greetings. A bit hearty.

"Not doing too badly," he said.

Could be that was an act, because he didn't look very glossy.

"Got an office round here?"

"It's in Orange Street."

I didn't know it was a turning point, not then, as I walked along to his office with him. Not with anything in mind, but just a feeling of "you never know your luck."

We passed the Comedy Theatre on the way. Paul's photograph had been blown up, since the publicity. One of those shots which made him look like a fretwork figure. Someone had been at the notices, and there was a banner across his legs saying, "One of our most promising young actors."

"I could do with a couple of those," Tony said.

"I know him."

"Well?"

I nodded. No good pushing it too much. I knew my Tony. "Come up to my office for a chat," he said.

The office was what they call a cold-water walk-up. Starts off with carpet, then linoleum and, when you got to his floor, nothing but bits of tin on the edge of the stairs. What good they do I don't know, except to break someone's neck coming down.

The outer office was like all outer offices. I knew them only too well. Girl with a typewriter, a sniff and a "no casting today" manner. And who should be sitting on a hard chair—the only chair, in a corner, but old Vic Jones, from Durrington. He was wearing his mackintosh. They don't usually heat the outer office. At least not so as you would notice. He looked just the same. Just as cheerful. It took a lot to get Vic down. I said hello, because I liked Vic and it's a dog's life being out of work. But before we could have a chat, I was swept in to the inner sanctum by Tony.

After a few seconds, Tony lifted the phone.

"Tell Vic Jones I shall be tied up for the rest of the afternoon, please."

"Yes, Mr. Banks." I heard the quack of the girl's voice. He put the phone down, and turned to me.

"It's no good having a lot of small names."

When you're small, you stay small, if you rely on the Tony Bankses of this world. We had a discussion about Paul, and ways and means of nobbling him from Everet without seeming to do so. I didn't mention any angle of my own. I know when to keep quiet. Anyway, it's best to look as if you don't need the money. It pays off in the end.

"Are you glad you packed in the acting?" I asked.

Tony looked at me, and smiled. He had a curiously boyish smile.

"I wasn't terribly good."

That was the thing about Tony, you couldn't dislike him, he was so honest about himself.

"Anyway," he went on, "I'm not good at the spitting and scratching bit."

"Paul's a spiky character."

It wasn't exactly a gypsy's warning, but I wasn't going to be involved. Not to the extent of carrying any cans back. He took no notice.

"Give me a ring if you can do anything, dear boy."

I looked at him. He wasn't bad looking. Large brown sympathetic eyes, dark hair a bit thin for the young juvenile. Just as well he'd given up acting. He was about right for an agent.

I didn't tell him I'd already spoken to Paul. Just as well to let people think you're giving them the big hand, because no credit is given where credit is due. You have to take it where you can find it. Grab it yourself.

A week later, we all met in a pub, a good way from the theatre, casually, of course. Just three friends meeting and chewing the fat over old times.

Paul and Tony took to one another. They were both in their charming mood. Both at their best, full of quips and sallies. Trying like hell. In spite of the fact that Paul was young, good looking and fair, and Tony fortyish, thickset and dark, they had something in common. Weakness, I think it was. Weakness and charm. Both success boys. Two peas in search of a gold-lined pod.

Still, I was glad they liked one another. I was able to slip away. I'd arranged the meeting between shows on a Saturday.

So I telephoned Shirley. She sounded pleased when I suggested coming round. The evenings are lonely for actors' wives. In some ways it's not a disadvantage.

When she opened the door to me at the flat, I felt the pang I'd felt the first day I'd seen her. She wasn't wearing her glasses and her gray myopic eyes peered at me. I felt the old, terrible wave of protectiveness. I say "terrible" because it was all I could do to prevent myself taking her in my arms, but that wouldn't do. Not yet.

As it was, I said, "Hello, Shirley."

"Charlie—darling, how nice to see you! Come in!"

The flat looked a bit better. There was a new armchair, a few pot plants scattered about. Naturally, most of them needed watering. The telly was on, but when I walked into the room Shirley turned it off immediately. There were a few baby clothes scattered about. The place looked cozy and homely, the curtains were drawn, the gas fire burning, although it was already early May. I gave her the tulips I'd brought with me. She went and put them in a vase immediately. Not many women do that. They like to make a business of flower arranging.

"I came round because I wanted to tell you Paul has met Tony Banks."

"Today?"

I nodded. "I introduced them and slipped away. I wanted to tell you about it. I think they'll suit one another."

"Wouldn't it be marvelous if he could do something for Paul?"

"Make a nice change."

"Paul gets so restless. It's difficult—when you have talent. It makes him edgy."

I knew all about the edgy bit. I wasn't sure about the talent. Not that it mattered. Plenty of swans swimming on the Avon are really ducks. No one has found out, that's all. We had supper together. Lots of laughs and friendship. An atmosphere you can't fake. Around eleven the child cried, and Shirley went into the bedroom to feed her.

When Paul rang, I opened the door to him. He seemed surprised to see me, and I made some good old Charlie noises: Shirley would like to know, hoped he'd got on all right with Tony, talent needs a boost. A load of old cobblers, but he sucked it up. That's the trouble with people who are, as the old joke has it, wrapped up in their own situation. They don't notice, fortunately. He said he'd got on all right, thought that he and Tony would join up.

Then he asked irritably, "Where's Shirley?" He might as well have said, "Where's my supper?"

"Feeding the baby."

We were standing in the hall. On the wall was an old spotted Victorian mirror, with gilt curlicues. Instinctively, he glanced into it. The bedroom door was open, and Shirley was sitting in front of the cheval glass. The two mirrors reflected one another.

Paul looked at Shirley and the baby, and I thought I knew what he was thinking. He'd told me before he hated all the processes of childbearing and feeding. The edges of his mouth showed disgust. Out of the corner of my eye I was looking in the mirror, too. I saw a woman bent tenderly over her child, the soft curve of her breast, the sucking child. To me, it was a classic madonna. I looked back at Paul King and felt a sudden upsurge of the old fears. The disgust had vanished from his expression. It was devoid of real emotion now, showing neither tenderness, pleasure, nor distaste, only a sort of cold speculation. It was the same expression he had had in the Durrington Theatre when he had been entertaining the new mayor, before he had married Shirley. If anything, it was a little more intense. On that occasion, only Shirley had been vulnerable. Now there was the child as well.

I made my excuses and left abruptly. There was nothing I could do. Nothing at all. Even more persistent was the memory of Jim Withers, with his cold eyes, saying, "I didn't say you could protect her. But you could avenge her. I said you could avenge her. If he's done it once, he can do it again—in a different way, of course."

10

One good turn, they say, deserves another, though it doesn't usually get one. This time, for once, and ironically, it did work out that way. I got Paul an agent, and he got me a job.

The publicity man for Paul's show was a nice queer. He didn't look queer. He looked more like a farmer. Maybe some farmers are queer, too. Everyone liked Mike Standford. They made as many excuses as they could for Mike. They needed to. He was always plastered. He was plastered on first nights when he should have been talking to the press, and he was recovering in the morning when he should have been sending off his hand-outs. But, as I said, people liked him. And that's not a bad quality in a publicity agent. After all, they are hired to be liked.

But Mike was getting to be a liability, he had pushed the boat out too often. He wasn't exactly sacked, but it was suggested by some clients that he needed an assistant. When Harvey Clinton, the management behind Paul's play, began to beef about him it was serious, because Clinton was currently Mike's chief meal ticket. It was the thick end of the wedge.

Paul suggested me. The money wasn't too good, but if the show eventually did well there was a cut on the profits, and it was a start for me.

Poor old Mike was an ex-actor, like me, "Honors Degree (failed)" stuff. He had a rabbit hole of a flat-cum-office off Shaftesbury Avenue. At one time he hadn't been doing too badly, until he took up with a male dancer, who ruined him and then left him flat, and broke too. Mike's reaction to love's disappointment was to hit the bottle. Shame really, because Mike was a nice man, a kind-hearted man, not cruel like some queers. It's like tarts, you get the kind-hearted kind, and the other sort who pinch your wallet while you're out for the count, though come to think of it, the same thing goes for non-queers, too.

I'd like to make it clear that I did not plan to ruin Mike. He'd got nothing else to live on, and anyway we got on all right. When I went into his dump, he was huddled over a smoky fire after an afternoon session. Obviously he had the father and mother of a hangover. He looked up at me, far from brightly.

"Are they going to out me?"

I thought it would save trouble if we got down to it straight away.

"I'm not going to out you," I said, "we'll play along together."

"You can easily dig a hole for me."

"I know. But I don't like digging. I don't like Harvey Clinton any more than you do." I'd always disliked him. He had a round pasty face like suet pudding, a fleshy body, a wet sensual mouth and some fluffy fawn hair, stuck on the back of his head like a crepe wig. I'd auditioned for him once, many years before. It's no fun auditioning at the best of times. Auditioning for Clinton made hell seem like a summer day. He played the actors like tickling trout. You could see the fear in their eyes, if they weren't in demand. And he chatted up the actresses. When I thought of him I could always see his wet tongue running across his wet mouth. I suppose some poor birds fell for his line. Though God knows you would have to be hard pressed to shack up with Clinton. I didn't like Clinton, but twenty quid a week is twenty quid a week.

"Why didn't Clinton out me?"

Mike looked up at me again. He could hardly lift his eyelids.

"I expect he values your experience," I said soothingly.

"Mind you," he mumbled on, "there's not a great deal to learn. It's just chatting people up, and getting angles. When I've had a couple of Alka's and a hair of the dog, I'll show you the cutting books. You'll soon get the hang of it. You'd better. I shan't last very long."

I thought it was a pretty hammy line, the old drunk playing for sympathy in the last reel. He finished his Alka Seltzer, and poured himself out a brandy, smoking and coughing. Between coughs, he went through his appointment book with me. He was no fool. As his nicotine-stained finger pointed out each name in the book, he would give a quick run-down of the man's character, weaknesses, vanities and obsessions.

"You have to be a bit of a psychologist to be in the publicity racket," he said. "Thing is, when I started in this game, it was just a question of getting the odd par in, bit of stuff on the first night, and for the women, a pic or two in the glossies. More complicated now. All this image building. We deal in images and personas, and all that crap."

He gave a wheezy laugh, and smiled at me, his expression good natured and a little sad.

"In the publicity racket—sorry, public relations—it's not what *is* that matters, but what *seems* to be. Get it? Give 'em a big hand, and keep your eyes skinned. You'll soon get to know the ropes," he repeated. "I'm tired. Think I'll go to bed."

He shambled off and turned in the doorway.

"Jessie—Mrs. Carter, comes around ten-thirty. I should turn up then if I were you. I'll give you a buzz if there's anything urgent this evening."

As I walked down the street after that first session with Mike, I knew that, at last, I had the means to destroy Paul's marriage. Publicity, the most destructive weapon of all to an actor—or to anybody else, come to that. I didn't think it had ever been done before. Not deliberately. The cool seeking of success for another in order to break his marriage. I knew the weaknesses at the root of the man I hated, I knew the strength of the weapon in my hand.

I would nurture the weaknesses until they smothered the man.

I recalled again the reason I had in Durrington for conceiving what I had facetiously called Operation Nut-Case: when the local boy makes good, he discards the girl he has married in the backwoods. He moves in a loftier rarefied atmosphere. Beautiful dolls sniff round him, younger, more sophisticated than his provincial wife.

Goodbye, wife. Nice to have seduced you. Sad I have to betray your trust, but you do understand, don't you?

I suppose that subconsciously I still had doubts about the theory of Brother Pete. Meanwhile, I had to learn to use my new armory of destruction.

11

Two months later, when the weapon was becoming smooth and comfortable to my hand I had a phone call in the early morning. Early for the theatre business, that is, a quarter past nine. A thick cockney voice said, "Hello?"

I was half asleep, and muttered sleepily, "Who's that?"

"Mrs. Wenham—from Mr. Standford's, Mr. Michael Standford," said the voice, louder and more insistently. "You better come, sir, he's queer, very queer."

She was right about that, but I felt no amusement, and knew from the urgency of her tone that when she said "queer," she meant dying. I got out of bed, dressed, and going down into the street found a cab, though that wasn't easy. At that time of the morning, a lot of people who were late for work were looking for cabs.

The office was in that maze of streets between Shaftesbury Avenue and the Charing Cross Road, run-down rabbit warren of a district, and the taxi driver kept on missing out on the one-way streets.

I went up the rickety stairs two at a time. Place was damp as hell and smelt of mice. Mrs. Wenham was standing at the head of the staircase in the darkness, a fat woman with a bashed-in face. She looked scared, and fright doesn't suit fat people.

"He's ever so queer," she said again, "can't seem to keep still."

I went through the untidy office into the bedroom. Mike was lying in a messy double bed. His eyes were shut and every now and again his body was shaken with half-conscious fits of shivering. Shuddering would be more like it, shuddering tremors, as if he were so cold that nothing could ever penetrate his blood with its warmth. His face had sunk in, and every few moments the shuddering took over, as if his body were having electric shocks through it. By the bedside was an empty whisky bottle and a glass.

"I put a hot water bottle in his bed."

Mrs. Wenham was behind me. He looked beyond hot water bottles to me. "I give him all the blankets I could find. He can't seem to get warm. I seen my old father like that. A rigor, I think the doctors called it."

She could call it what she liked, but it looked like death to me, not ordinary rigor.

"Have you sent for the doctor?"

"I didn't know what to do—is he on the National Health?"

"I've no idea."

"You work with him?"

She was reproachful, as if I ought to have his National Health Service Card in my pocket as part of the service.

"Oh, dear, gentlemen on their own do find it difficult to manage."

Poor old Mike, he was a gentleman on his own, all right. He'd been on his own ever since the dancer walked out. The breathing from the bed had become sharp and painful to listen to. I went into the next room and, after I'd tried my own doctor, who was out, I rang the police. They gave the name of another doctor in the district. Reluctantly and after some brisk exchanges, he said he'd come round. Mrs. Wenham and I waited.

"D'you like a cup of tea?"

I said, yes. I would. Poor old girl, she wanted something to do. She looked at the man on the bed.

"I don't suppose we ought to give him anything—doctors don't always like them to have anything. Not if they haven't suggested it, do they?" She had that old-fashioned respect for doctors which went out with top hats.

"I don't think he could take anything, not at the moment," I murmured.

"I did make him a cuppa tea earlier, but he didn't touch it."

I noticed it on the night table. The milk had congealed on the top, and it looked brown and nasty.

"I'll get your tea," she said, "and I've got a few biscuits. I always like to have biscuit with my elevenses."

The mind clings to trivialities when faced with death, to prove one is still alive, and Mrs. Wenham was clinging to her biscuits to prove she still existed. By the time she'd put the tea in the office, the doctor arrived, a young, fresh-faced chap obviously not long out of medical school. His health and good humor seemed to make the whole set-up, the flat, the dying man, the congealing tea, more sordid than ever. I drank my tea in the office while he examined Mike. He came out of the bedroom, shutting the door quietly, and the sound of the shuddering and dreadful breathing was muffled.

"What's the matter with him?"

"Can't quite make him out. He could be heading for pneumonia, but the main trouble is his heart. You a relation?"

I shook my head.

"Close friend?"

"Not really. Business colleague."

He looked round the shoddy office, with its atmosphere of failure and then at me, connecting the two, and not to my advantage.

"Shouldn't we get him to hospital?" I suggested coldly.

"You mean oxygen tents, and all the rest. Might be worth a try, if we could get a bed, but on the whole, it's not worth it." He was young enough not to be moved by the death of a failure. "Anyway, if I moved him, he'd probably conk out. He's in bad shape. Obviously an alcoholic."

"What do you suggest?"

My voice was harsh. His overflowing good humor and good health irritated me. When you're young you think you can never be old or ill, or even a failure.

"I'll send some oxygen round here, and a nurse if I can rustle one up. If you ask me, I'd say he wouldn't last long, but I could be wrong. How long has he been like this?"

"Couple of hours—maybe longer, the 'daily' found him."

"Drunks always go quickly when they start to go."

He looked round the tatty office again. I could see he

94

was wondering what the hell kind of business we carried on from that dump.

"I'll send the nurse round. I've got a couple of girls who'll usually help out—if they're free."

"Thanks."

"Don't worry—you've done your best."

The doctor went out, into the street where the sun was shining, and there was no smell of death. I went in and sat beside Mike. After half an hour or so, the shudders slowed down.

"You there, Charlie?" He didn't open his eyes. I suppose he knew my step.

"Yes."

"Told you I wouldn't last long. Life's—"

I made some reassuring noises as he broke off. His body was racked with another series of tremors.

"Life's bloody—I'm not afraid, not afraid at all. Fed up with grunting and sweating." He lay back on his pillows and said nothing for a minute.

Then he said, "Nothing much to live for, you know. Used to think life was a ball." He gave a sort of wheeze which could have been a laugh. "That ball rolled away all right."

His voice grew softer, and I could no longer hear what he was saying. It seemed an endless muttering which went on and on, like a tape running backwards. The nurse knocked at the door just at the moment Mike died. I could see she was quite relieved that the assignment had been so short, it wasn't the sort of place she would have liked to work in. Don't blame her. She was a tall rangy Australian girl, just the doctor's type.

Jessie Carter, the secretary, came in half an hour later. She came in carrying her shopping, which she did in the market on the way. I could see some lettuce sticking out of the bag. She worried about her figure. She was an ex-chorus girl, must have been about thirty-three, with auburn hair and a pale face.

She put down her shopping, and said, "Mike got a hang-over, as usual?"

She took the cover off her typewriter. For a moment I didn't know how to tell her. It was hard to break the normality and ordinariness of the morning. Still, it was no good beating about the bush and wrapping it up.

"Mike's dead. He died half an hour ago. I've sent for the undertaker."

Her face went even more colorless. She stood with the dusty mackintosh typewriter cover in her hand, stared and said, "How did it happen?"

"I don't know. I think it was his heart."

"Did you get a doctor?"

I reassured her, and she sat down on her typing chair with the tears oozing out of her eyes, like taps dripping. Quite expressionless.

"It's so sad, a queer dying," she said. "Terrible, he leaves nothing behind, nothing at all."

They say everyone has to have someone to weep for them in order to be forgiven. Mike had two. I was crying inside. After a few seconds, I went and cried outside, too, in the lavatory. Howled like a wolf. We're given tear glands, might as well use them.

Not many came to the cremation. Just one or two publicity people. It's not very cheerful seeing someone go up in smoke. Jessie and I thanked them for coming, and then we walked away together. The ex-dancer and the ex-actor, the only two who really saw the curtain down. I got a paragraph about his death into the evening papers, mentioned that he had been doing the publicity for Paul's show, thereby getting a bit more publicity for it. Professional touch. Mike would have approved. Showed I had learnt the job.

After the cremation I took Jessie out to lunch. I knew she minded about Mike. She'd been propping him up for so long that she'd miss him more than I did.

"What about his things—the flat—everything?"

She looked at me, surprised, and raised thin, old-fashioned eyebrows, the kind you sometimes see in old movies.

"He said he wanted you to carry on, if anything happened to him. I thought you knew?"

"What about you?"

"He gave me some money a couple of years ago, when my husband left me flat broke."

"Didn't he have any relations?"

"Never heard of any. Queers sometimes cut adrift from their relations."

Jessie looked at me. She was still very pretty.

"You know, you may think the business isn't much, but it could be a good one if it were run right. Mike drank away the profits, but there's a lot of money in publicity. We could do people as well as shows. We could sell the lease of the flat. Mike didn't want to move, he couldn't be bothered. We could get ourselves a smarter office. If we sold the lease it would make a down payment. You need a bit of front in this business."

I nodded, knowing she was speaking the truth.

"Poor old Mike—after Gerald left him, he never seemed to get to grips again. He'd give you his last bean. I know. We'd get quite a bit for the lease," she insisted. "There's still twenty years to go."

We did indeed get quite a bit for the lease. It gave us a nice bit of working capital, and we rented a couple of rooms in one of those glass beehives which are going up all over the place. The rooms were small, but it had a good entrance with a fountain and rubber plants. As Jessie said, you have to have a bit of front.

I had my name printed on the door. "charles maither—publicity." Stark, modern stuff. No capital letters. Nothing fancy. Good thing I was called Maither. It had a nice publicity ring about it. Not that I had any connection with the Mather advertising people. None at all. Pure coincidence. But helpful, very helpful indeed.

Jessie got in her niece as secretary. Nice girl, good natured, with a large bosom, called Pam. Pam had wanted to go on the stage, but with her face and that bosom Jessie had persuaded her against it. She was useful in the office, though, and thought show business was wonderful. Starry eyed, but helpful. Ideal combination.

We managed to get a couple more shows on the books.

Now that she could get out and about, instead of having to cover up for Mike's hangovers, Jessie turned out to be a good saleswoman, very good for the job. She knew a lot of people, and they all liked her. You never know where your talents lie. Good old Jessie—and good old me.

Meanwhile, Paul's show continued to do well, but there wasn't much news in it. No one seemed to be having babies, breaking legs, or getting divorced; none of the routine bread-and-butter stuff of the publicity game.

I wasn't seeing much of Paul and Shirley, but on the last occasion I had noted an atmosphere of suppressed excitement. It was particularly noticeable in Shirley, though even Paul didn't look as moody as usual. But they were being cagey, playing it close to the chest, even with me. Theatre people are like that. As a shot in the dark, I asked jocularly if any film offers were around. Breezy old Charlie stuff.

I saw Shirley's eyes light up, but Paul gave her a hard look and answered for both of them. "I'll let you know about things in due course. Meanwhile don't start any rumors about anything at all, Charlie."

I agreed, but naturally I went round to see Tony Banks the very next day. I wasn't going to lie down under that sort of provocative nonsense. Either Paul trusted me as a friend, or he didn't. I mean, you ought to trust your friends.

Tony had moved offices, too. We were all going up in the world. He'd rented a bit of an old house in Mayfair; antique desk and pine fireplace. Trad stuff. It suited him. He seemed pleased to see me. It was easy to see the gravy was beginning to come in. I sat down and refused a cigar.

"I heard something about a film for Paul," I said flatly.

"There's quite a few things on the stocks."

"Paul needs a boost."

I used Shirley's words, but privately I was thinking that what he really needed was a damned great boost into outer space, on a non-returnable basis.

"I agree with you, dear boy. Entirely."

"There's nothing much to do for his present show. Nothing new. Or is there?"

He looked up at me, wondering how much I'd heard.

He said, "No good starting rumors if there's nothing in them."

"Not for publication—I promise."

"Silent as the grave?"

"Agreed."

He decided to trust me, and said, "Paul wasn't signed for the run of the play. He's leaving to rehearse a new one in a couple of weeks. I got the okay today."

I said Tony was good about contracts. The get-out clause is something people can overlook. It's no good getting buried too long in a success. People forget you.

"And the film?" I said, still shooting in the dark.

"In the air—but the smell of dinner is about."

"Glad to hear it."

Tony had that little edge of satisfaction, something like a punter who has backed the right horse. We looked at one another.

"What's the new play?"

He told me. It was called *Deeper in the South*. I had heard about it. Kind of sub-Tennessee Williams. It had been a success in New York. Managements like buying up something ready-made. Saves bother. They call it a property. Sounds solid, of course. Comes to them ready-made, with the glitter on. Success insured, they think. Sometimes the glitter drops off in mid-Atlantic. Doesn't stop them doing it again.

"And the film?"

"Depends on the success of the play."

"Don't you think it would be a good idea for Paul to have a little personal publicity—apart from the play?"

"He's had quite a bit."

"I know, but that was the new young star angle." I had to play it carefully here. "What you want is the serious actor bit. Something much more prestigey."

"What would it cost?" Tony had a firm grip on the essentials. I put on my good-natured, helpful expression.

"Well—you know Paul and I are old friends. What I suggest is that—if the reviews are good—I could do a little personal campaign for, say, a hundred pounds."

"That's very cheap."

"I know. But I realize, and so do you, that this could be the turning point. And he *is* my friend."

"Okay, *if* the notices are good."

"Is the play good?"

"I'll let you read it, but I don't want any releases about it till the rehearsals are under way. The cast isn't fixed yet."

He didn't have to tell me my job, but I smiled and he handed me the play. *Deeper in the South*—sounded like that good old oldie about the color problem. English actors are hell when they get stuck with the mammy accent.

"And the film?" I said again. I could feel that Tony wasn't coming quite clean over the film.

"It's a kind of loose contract with Enterprise."

"Joe Gross?"

He nodded and added, "Nice little man." That put old Joe in his place.

But Joe really was a nice little man. His parents had come over from Poland in the 'twenties, and his mother wanted him to be a rabbi, because rabbis have a more settled way of life, so he became a film producer. Short, small, very Jewish looking, but with it a way of caricaturing his own race which had something endearing. I liked Joe.

"Joe's a real chum," said Tony. This meant Joe wasn't smarter than Tony, not when it came to the small print. "Joe's thinking of making it during the run of the play."

"That'll be helpful with the campaign."

I'd got the whole picture now. We only needed to paint it rosier than it was, and the job was half done.

"Paul actually signed up?"

"Not yet."

This meant small print was being read and fought over.

"Ring me when you've read the play. I'd like to know what you think."

Why should he care?

"Of course. Who's the director?"

"American called Harry Alvarez. Super-method boy, full of overcharged batteries."

He didn't sound the right man for Paul.

"He has a splendid reputation. But it's a tough part."

Tony's expression was shrewd. Weighing up the reputation against Paul's acting. The heavy going against the horse's record. When I read the script, I knew Tony was right. Maybe Paul could do it. Maybe.

On the way back to the office, I ran into old Vic Jones in the Charing Cross Road. He looked just the same and always seemed pleased to see me, which made a change. I didn't ask him if he was in work.

"Funny meeting you," he said. "I'm just off to give Sarah a bit of coaching. You remember Sarah Barnes from Durrington?"

"Of course. Good actress."

"Very good."

"What's Sarah doing?"

"She did that piece at the Arts, then she was out for a bit, then a couple of tellys, and now she's up for *Deeper in the South,* a new American play. Sensitive young wife stuff. Highly emotional, but she can do it on her head. She's twenty-seven but she can play down to twenty, easily."

There were going to be fireworks at rehearsal. Paul wasn't going to like this. She might easily walk away with the notices.

"Hear you're in the publicity game now," he said. "Given up the business?"

"It gave me up. Did the publicity for Paul's show at the Comedy."

He smiled gently and said, "What an ordinary little piece that is! I got a couple of comps. Couldn't get them now. Just shows you the power of the box."

He wasn't being catty, just objective.

"Paul's still giving the same performance, too," he added.

I didn't agree or disagree. I just left the thing in the air. No good fouling your own nest.

"Still, it's a good performance, in its way—pity to waste it!"

Vic smiled. Good-humored chap, Vic. Salt of the outer office. He read my thoughts.

"Tony Banks was a waste of time for me." It was his only

reference of our previous brush. "He's after the big boys. I haven't got an agent now. Waste of time till you've made it."

It was one of those conversations. Kind of petered out for lack of steam. I'd have liked to do something for him. What? Ten per cent of nothing is nothing. I couldn't help. I had my own troubles.

With a couple of desultory "see you's" we parted, and I watched him going down the street. Mackintosh flapping, head bent against the wind, dispatch case under his arm. Oddly optimistic. Nice man, Vic Jones. Fat lot of good that is.

A couple of weeks later rehearsals started.

As I said, we'd all gone up in the world and not only with offices, but with houses; not much but a little, in the sense that we'd left our sleazy lodgings. I had a three-roomed flat in the wilderness, near the Cromwell Road. Basement and darkness, but better than the Battersea hole.

Paul and Shirley had a temporary flat in Earls Court, while they looked for something more permanent.

Meanwhile, Paul's new play was to tour for six weeks, and Shirley thought she might take a cottage for the rest of the summer. I agreed with her. I even offered to put up Paul in my flat during rehearsals. Nice of me, I thought. As I said to Shirley, "I shall be able to help him. Keep up his morale. And he'll be on tap for interviews, too. Never too soon to start building up the image."

Publicity people are right when they call it an image. It has nothing to do with reality. When you call somebody a silly old image, you may be nearer the truth than you think.

The rehearsals were tougher on Paul than suited my purpose. It was no part of my plan for him to be a poor thing.

Some directors think that if they bang an actor flat, like schnitzel, they'll get the best out of him. There are actors who can do with the schnitzel treatment, but I didn't think Paul was one of them.

"A flop don't do no one no good," as Joe Gross used to say, least of all my budding publicity business. I was a little worried. I could often hear Paul pacing up and down

102

and muttering his part. This was where I did a bit of standing in for Shirley.

One night, after a week of rehearsals, I knocked at his door. He was sitting on the bed looking like Hamlet. Not that Paul would have cared about his father's ghost. I went up to him and gripped his shoulders with that speechless sincerity I am so good at. For a long moment I said nothing. A pause is as good as a speech.

"You're worried," I said at last, as if I'd just found out.

He nodded. He'd still got his "little boy lost" expression, a lock of hair falling into his eyes, the look that goes down so well with the women.

"You're good, you're very good!" I said, still in tones of ringing sincerity. "Remember that!"

He looked up at me thoughtfully. Maybe I had overdone it. So I looked away, the old chum overcome with emotion.

"Alvarez seems to have taken quite a shine to Sarah," he said at last.

He had, and it was not surprising. She was much better than Paul. Also she took direction. I said, still looking at him with my sympathetic friend look, "Alvarez *asked* for you. Why?"

I paused there, and said in tones of even greater ringing sincerity: "Because he thinks you are *good!*"

This seemed to convince him. It agreed with his own opinion, and it is always nice to have one's feelings about oneself confirmed by an intelligent friend.

Meanwhile, Jessie and I were playing the publicity fairly cool. Little bit in the *Sunday Times,* short bit in the *Observer,* something about the new trend in plays in the *Spectator.* We were playing down the women's stuff at this stage. I felt more and more strongly that Paul should be taken up as a serious actor. He wasn't, and never would be. But no one except me knew that.

The Sunday before the show went on tour, Shirley telephoned and asked me to come to lunch at their country cottage. I'd rather have waited till Paul was out of the way.

"Wouldn't you like to have the day with Shirley?" I asked Paul, turning from the phone. He shook his head and said we could drive down together. I wondered whether he was saving the train fare. He hadn't got a car. No good buying one until he could get something with a bit of class. He knew that.

I was wrong about the train fare. When we got to the cottage, his mother Edith was there. No wonder he wanted a buffer. She was alleged to be in need of a rest. My opinion was that it was the women with whom she worked who wanted a month off from Edith.

The cottage was uncomfortable, and Edith was sitting in the only decent chair. Rolling a cigarette with her machine, as usual, the ash drooping from her current cigarette.

"You're here," she said. "Paul, you *do* look done up." Cheerful old thing, as usual.

"Where's Shirley?" Paul asked irritably.

"In the garden with the baby. She doesn't seem able to manage her. Some women make such a business of being mothers."

Paul looked through the cottage window to where Shirley was wheeling Jane under the trees. I could see he agreed with Edith. In a way, Edith was on my side, although she didn't know it. She was a good hand at attacking on the soft underbelly. Paul didn't like the attention taken off himself, by a baby or anything else. He opened a window and called out. He wasn't in a very good mood now. Can't blame him. On hearing his voice, Shirley tucked the child up and ran across the grass towards the cottage. The sun and the fresh air had touched her cheeks with color.

"I didn't hear the car," she said as she kissed Paul, and then brushed my cheek with her lips. It was wonderful to see her. Paul wasn't thinking that. Not to judge by his expression. Shirley poured out sherries.

"Has Tony rung up?" asked Paul.

"No," Shirley replied, "are you expecting him to?"

"You know damn well I am."

"Is it about the film?" I asked. If Paul was fidgety, it could only be about his own prospects. He nodded.

"If he hasn't phoned, the contract has probably fallen

through," said Edith, taking a slug of sherry. Dear old thing, really. Shirley had tears in her eyes.

"You know what it is," I said quickly, "most people don't do much from Friday to Monday."

Shirley went out to the kitchen to dish up. I went with her. She stood by the sink, tears rolling down her cheeks.

I put an arm round her shoulders, and said, "Don't pay any attention to Edith. Bloody old raven."

"Paul needs this film, *really* needs it," she said.

Now I don't want to give the impression that Shirley talked about nothing but Paul. She did touch lightly upon other subjects. Now and again. But I had to put up with a good deal. Paul needs a bit of luck. Paul needs a chance. Paul needs a boost. Paul needs a film. Who doesn't? Sometimes it nearly made me sick. But I couldn't be snappy with her now, standing over the sink with tear-wet cheeks, the soppy angel.

Her short-sighted eyes peered at me anxiously. He didn't deserve her. That was always my justification, even before the talk with Jim Withers. Lunch wasn't much of a success. I could see Paul waiting for the phone to ring. I knew all about phone calls, the kind that never came, don't ring us, we'll ring you.

But at two o'clock, it rang. Edith's face fell. Tony arrived by car about teatime. Each time I saw him, he seemed a bit glossier. He greeted me briefly. Big stuff on hand. No time to toss more than a word to the peasants.

"My dear chap," he said to Paul, "I think we're beginning to see daylight!" Paul's expression lightened.

"If we play our cards right, this is only the beginning!" I was thinking the same.

He accepted a drink and they went off into a long discussion about options to renew, contingency emergencies, the sale of further rights in Paul. I could hear Shirley making tea in the kitchen. Paul had the usual dedicated expression of someone who is absorbed in his own concerns. Tony said, "I'm thinking of putting a small clause in the contract; we don't want to tie you down too firmly with Joe Gross."

"Let's come out into the garden," murmured Paul. I could

feel he had been trying to edge me out of the room, and I didn't feel like being edged. I was getting to know his expressions very intimately by now. Like a close-up camera. They went out into the garden. The flowers smelled sweet. Birds sang. The sun shone. Bees droned. I saw their two figures, bent together, deep in discussion of contracts. Nature could wait. Money is a serious and sincere subject.

When Shirley called them in to tea, they were looking very pleased with one another. It had been decided that Paul should sign, that Tony's little clause should be slipped in. He would make one film during the run of the play, if all went well.

"It makes all the difference, having a good agent," said Paul. He was looking pleased for a change. Events were further confirming his own opinion about himself. "You've done very well," he added.

Tony preened himself. He was full of the joys of spring now, birds, bees, the lot. That was one thing about Tony, he did like to report successes. The fact that he disappeared over the nearest horizon as soon as the rot set in didn't alter that fact. Anyway, there's nothing like hitching your wagon to a rising star.

Later, Paul said again, "It makes all the difference having a good agent."

I thought of Vic Jones. I even thought of myself. Gulls don't follow empty rowing boats. Nor do agents.

Like everything else, first nights always sound better in the gossip columns. *Deeper in the South* was no exception. I was in the foyer. Doing my good old Charlie act in a sixty-guinea dinner jacket, hire purchase, tax deductible. There was a mild powdering of mink in the stalls. Little black dresses and stoles in the circle. Not what you'd call your smash-hit audience. I could see Tony thought the same thing when he arrived.

His eyes were flicking round. He had a redhead with him. Slim girl with green eyes, wearing pink. Some redheads like to do that. It draws attention to their hair. Hers was very long. That careless-careful style. She kept turning her head so that it fell this way and that, hoping to net something, possibly one of Tony's up-and-comings.

"Hello, hello," I said. An original remark.

"Hello, Charlie. Do you know Stella Fenton? Charlie's doing the publicity for the show." I needed my price tag.

The redhead's expression improved when she heard the word "publicity." She was in show business all right. Another flick of the red hair, and very nice too, if you appreciate that sort of thing.

"Seen Paul?" I asked Tony. He nodded.

"He's nervous, of course."

"All the best actors are," said Stella, to show she knew all about it.

The bell rang. Seconds out. The house lights dimmed. It's always a moment which grips your stomach. First night dramas are always tense. Difficult to tell how they are going. Is the applause polite, from friends and relations, or is the play cracking through to the inner core, to the pros? Comedies are easier. Either they are sitting on their hands, or laughing. You can't fake real laughter.

I wasn't sure about *Deeper in the South*. Still, no one was coughing. Extraordinary how quickly bronchitis spreads when an audience is bored.

Paul was giving his usual performance. Helped by the tough American dialogue, and by Sarah. Child brides are hell, but she gave it something she had learned in the outer office. Lost illusions and opportunities missed.

I didn't see the whole play. I was too busy entertaining the Press and chatting-up useful people. They seemed well-disposed, though you never know, not till the papers arrive in the morning. You can't hear a tone of voice in print.

I went round soon after curtain down. From the number of people buzzing round Paul's dressing room, it looked as if he were well in. So I popped along to congratulate Sarah, and found her with her mouth open, dabbing her gums with oil of cloves.

"Poor darling," said a large woman I had never seen before, "she's had raging toothache the whole evening."

"Was I awful?" croaked Sarah, holding her mouth half open.

"No, darling, you were wonderful." And for once I meant it.

"Is it going to be all right?"

"I gave her a reassuring pat, and muttered more praise.

"Shirley here?" I asked.

Sarah shook her head. "The baby had a temperature at the last minute."

Poor old Shirley, she was getting the worst of both worlds. The dressing room was starting to fill up now, and I know when to make myself scarce. In the passage outside I ran into Vic.

"Coming to see Sarah?" Vic looked surprised at my question.

"Didn't she tell you? She got me in as an understudy. Someone went down with appendicitis."

One man's appendix is another man's meal ticket. Vic looked gloomy. I wondered why. After all, he was in work.

"Anything the matter?"

"Bit of contract trouble. They haven't signed me for the run of the play."

Funny, really. Successes, like Paul, want a get-out clause, and the others want to eat regularly. I walked round to the front of the theatre and saw Paul's name up in lights. It was a beginning.

I was in a pretty low state when I left the Builders' Arms. The return visit to Durrington was doing me no good at all. The past was rushing through my mind, not always in detail, of course, as I have set it out above, but sometimes in a cascade of general recollection and sometimes in snatches and brief sequences, bits and pieces of scenes and odd sentences from conversations long past and always, of course, coming back to the police—and the rest of the bitter, painful story.

Dr. Maynard had suggested I should go back, wrapping up the suggestion in a medley of psychological theories typi-

cal of his convoluted Viennese mind. I think he was getting fed up with me, though not with my money. I suppose he had to go on producing something for my money.

So far from doing me good, I was feeling worse. I was even developing secondary guilt complexes about other characters.

Such as Tony Banks, and what happened to him.

12

The next morning, I went out to get the papers at about eight o'clock. Nobody need have worried about the play. The notices were all good. I spread them out on my desk and looked at them with grim satisfaction. Paul had been hailed as a splendid actor, which he wasn't. This happens all the time—actors getting the credit for the play, or siphoning off some credit from another actor. In this case it was Sarah. But Paul was still a new face, and people like a new face in the lead, gives them something to write about.

I took Paul the papers about nine o'clock. Actors are always unconscious till eleven but this was a special occasion. He was still dead asleep, his face expressionless and blank. I suppose he was handsome, with his fair hair spread out on the pillow, and that profile.

It was the blank expression which suddenly fascinated me. Most people have softening lines or contours, even when asleep. His was a face totally devoid of mercy or pity. I couldn't help it, I didn't want to think about such things, but I felt an awful speculation about how it would feel to have Paul King's face as the last face one saw, the heart pounding with fear, and all hope vanishing, and yet again all hope vanishing, in seconds, and only Paul King's face. But of course it wouldn't be blank and expressionless.

I felt the little hairs tickling my neck, because like most actors, I reckon I can get inside somebody else's skin, even a strangled woman's. There were long periods when I forgot Jim Withers and Brother Pete. But there was no reason why a killer should not be an actor.

I always came back to that.

Thus, I watched him for some seconds, and when the horror images had passed, I woke him.

"Relax! They are all good!" I said boisterously. I was looking terribly pleased and proud.

He was one of those people who wake up slowly, as if they have been drugged. He took the papers, and without any change of expression read them all. Sarah was good, but he'd walked away with the play, that was the theme.

"Congratulations, boyo!" I said. "Splendid! Couldn't be better!"

"Thanks, Charlie."

He was accepting his success, as if he had always known it would happen. He added, with a complacent note in his voice, which I was glad to hear, "I always knew—even when I was at Durrington—that I was different."

Too true he was different. But it must be good to feel that nature has picked you out for the "A" stream of life, that destiny has pointed with a finger and said, "You!" Or is it good?

"I wouldn't say that to anyone except you, Charlie."

It's natural to trust a friend. I smiled.

"All you will have to worry about now is—success!"

"That's an easy one." Then, suddenly, he became thoughtful. He lit a cigarette and sat on the edge of the bed, with the newspapers spread around him, staring at the floor, and made what to me was a frightening and, though I hated the bastard, an almost pathetic remark.

"I've got this—something. Something inside me. Do you think we can fight against our destiny, Charlie? Do you think there's an outside influence over which we have no control—whether we're successful or not? Is the drunkard responsible for his alcoholism?"

I stared at him, then looked away.

"He can develop will power to fight it, if he wants to," I muttered.

"What if he hasn't got the wish to fight it? How do you breed a desire to fight it, Charlie?"

"You're not a drunk," I said, feebly.

"No, I'm not a drunk," he agreed. "I'm not a drunk. Well, let's say I don't take alcohol much. It's just that now I seem to be on the way up and I don't want to spoil it. It would be a pity to—oh! forget it."

He stopped and shook his head, almost despairingly.

"Pity to what?" I pressed him.

"Nothing."

"I'm your friend."

Whatever he had done in the past, it was the future that mattered. I couldn't have blood upon my hands, or so I thought. I began to gather the newspapers together; thinking, maybe and perhaps, perhaps and maybe.

Finally, I took a sort of modified plunge and said, "Look, if you're worried about anything personal, why not have a chat with somebody?"

"With whom?" he asked, suspiciously.

"Psychoanalysts are all the rage in America, especially in the acting profession—get swinging, be trendy!" I said hastily, with a sort of ghastly jocularity.

"How can I afford it?" he said uncertainly. "They cost the earth, these bloody types."

"You're on the way up, you're going to be well off," I said loudly, "be happy as well!"

He picked at a blanket. I could almost hear his brain going tick-tock, tick-tock. Outside, an electrically driven milk van went humming by and for about twenty seconds I thought he might agree but then he said, well, he'd see, he'd think about it, and that meant no.

Nobody can say I didn't do my best.

By midday, Tony Banks was on the blower naturally full of the joys of spring. Joe Gross had better watch the small print, I thought. I went back to the office in the afternoon. Jessie was hard at work.

"A girl called Stella Fenton has been ringing you."

111

"Never heard of her."

"She said she met you with Tony Banks, last night." I remembered her then.

Jessie raised her old-fashioned plucked eyebrows.

"Another client?"

"Possibly," I said. "She's a shrewd pussy. She may lead to something."

Stella Fenton came to see me the following day. She was a sharp flint all right. And ambitious. Tony Banks had fixed her up with a small film contract, and she wanted a little publicity. She hadn't had much experience, six months in Rep, and a couple of stints. I wondered how she managed to look so sleek on that kind of business, and thought acidly that it was no concern of mine.

I was wrong. She lived with her mother in Chelsea. Mother had money, and she was staking Stella. Stella didn't lay anything out on the line on spec, not even her virtue, just as Paul didn't fling his money about.

And you could say that again. Paul was still living with me. Five pounds a week bed and breakfast and what he could scrounge from the fridge. He didn't even bring in an occasional bottle of wine. I was getting a bit fed up with him. He had begun working on the film during the day, and was in the play at night. He was hard worked all right, and knew it. Giving a good performance of being an overworked genius. Much better than he gave in the evenings. Having him around was a bore, keeping up the good old Charlie performance. Nevertheless, once or twice I thought I caught a brooding look about him, and on one occasion, when I myself came in late, he was on the telephone and lowered his voice, ringing off almost at once.

I did not suspect anything sinister. I suspected something professional. Actors sometimes go on like this. They're superstitious about discussing a new project in the offing. I asked no questions.

Sarah Barnes gave a party the Sunday after the hundredth performance. It was a milestone for her, the first time she had acted so long in a success. I arrived very late, if the ash

trays were anything to go by. There were quite a lot of people there. They'd got to the stage of sitting on the floor. It
seemed a good party. No drunks and no one being sick in
the bathroom. All the cast were there. At first I couldn't
see Paul.

Then I did see him. Odd sometimes how a scene is caught
in your mind, like a sudden shot in a film. I looked across
the room and saw him. He was laughing in an uninhibited
way, as if he'd forgotten about Paul King for a moment,
and that was a bloody miracle in itself.

I couldn't see the girl beside him, then she moved into
the light. It was Stella. As she turned away, Paul followed
her with his eyes. Like a child peering into a toy shop window. But not so innocent. Just greedy. I was interested in
that look. Then I heard Tony's voice.

"There you are, Charlie! Has Paul said anything to you?"

"I've only just arrived."

"I suppose you've heard he's been offered three years
at Stratford-on-Avon?"

"Stratford?" I said, amazed. An offer from the Shakespeare
Memorial Theatre was serious stuff.

I remembered the brooding look and surreptitious phone
call, and felt the old sharp pang of professional envy shoot
through me, but decided to play it cool.

"What do you think? After all, he might get other film
offers."

"True, true, too true," Tony said.

Tony was thinking it out. So far, only the small film fish,
like Joe Gross, had been biting. But it wouldn't suit my book
or Tony's if Paul became a dedicated stage actor.

"I've never thought that Paul has *quite* the depth for
Shakespeare. Still, I could be wrong," I said in the good old
well-tried Confidential Pal tone, though it lost some effect
because I had almost to shout to make myself heard. I
shrugged my shoulders, but I could see that I'd nurtured the
seed in Tony's mind.

"Stratford is a world stage," he roared, above the din
of the party.

His expresssion did not suggest a man entirely devoted to the arts, because unfortunately there is this eternal struggle between art and making the fast fiver for the rent.

"What do you think, yourself?" he asked me, still speaking loudly, above the noise of the party. He looked at me, a dog asking for a bone.

"I would hesitate," I shouted, "to give advice on anyone's career."

"He hasn't said anything to you?" I shook my head. Several people were leaving, and we lowered our voices.

"Perhaps you could put in a word?"

"The best word would be if someone came up with a good film offer," I said. "But he's tied to Joe Gross."

"Not all that tied," said Tony Banks, carefully.

He had the dedicated look of someone who is doing sums of money in his head. I could see he hadn't forgotten his small clause.

"Three years is a long time."

I said this slowly, letting the idea of the appalling length of three years in a show-biz career sink into his mind.

Where it stayed, for the run of the play.

I spent some of my time promoting Stella Fenton. She was very photogenic, so it wasn't difficult. I even introduced her to Joe Gross, who gave her a couple of small bits.

Some Saturdays I went down to the country to keep Shirley company. The baby was walking now, and a pretty little thing Jane was, dark and animated, and very fond of me, unless she was a better actress than her parents.

Shirley had come to rely on me in small ways, She was getting used to me, and to the fact that I was often around. We were on an easy intimate footing. Sometimes she'd laugh and say I ought to get married. I'd say, yes I would, when I met the right girl.

"You're such a *nice* man, Charlie," she said one day. So I was—with her. She brought out the best in me, and, in a way, the worst, and you can underline that.

You know how it is, you can feel when a woman is lonely, and likes to have another man around. It is an opportunity.

Looking at her there in the garden that day, in the late sunshine, it was hard not to tell her I wanted to *give,* and that Paul was a man who always took. There could never be an end to his taking. I knew it for a disease.

"You never know, someone may have me."

"Probably. People have very bad taste," she said fondly. So the scene ended in friendly laughter, and we went in to lunch.

Of course, we discussed Paul's career during the meal. All the old dedication crap. I pointed out to her that if he got a really big film offer and accepted it, he would only take it because he was thinking of her and Jane. Dear old Charlie, spreading sweetness and light about his old friend.

"Actors don't get pensions," I said earnestly. "They have to think of the future. People forget that."

"I wouldn't want to stand in his way. I have never done that."

Dear Shirley. How she clung to the myth of Paul. It was not time to disillusion her.

Meanwhile, back at the inn, as they say, Paul and Tony were engaged in a ding-dong battle. Tony had jacked Joe Gross and the film company up to fifty thousand, and was trying to prove that it was in the greater cause of art for Paul to sign a firm contract for a new film.

I could feel Paul's indecision. Like a dog between two juicy bones, he was uncertain which one to snap up. Lucky old Rover.

I was still doing Paul's publicity for the film of *Deeper in the South,* and the publicity was going well. The cuttings in my black book were mounting. Double spreads, interviews, Paul's views about acting, Paul's views about every aspect of the Drama from the Greeks to the present day, with a condescending nod at Shakespeare on the way.

"Why do you trouble to stick the cuttings in yourself?" Jessie asked me. "We can get Pam to do it."

"I feel Paul is my baby," I said, with a tender smile. Some baby.

I liked to watch the cuttings grow, to see the subtle changes which success was making in his face. From the phoney, sunny boyish expression of the early shots to the phoney "dedicated artist" of the later ones, and how the lines of self-absorption were growing. There is always a point when the victim starts to believe his own hand-outs. He had not quite reached that watershed yet, but it was coming. The shadow was on his face.

Tony was very pleased with the job I was doing. It helped with the film contracts, helped to nudge the price up. Publicists don't have to believe in the product. We all know that the face that launched a film contract will be wrapping up the fish tomorrow.

But I had miscalculated.

I had forgotten about the underlying dislike which Paul and Sarah Barnes had for each other, dating right back to the old Durrington days, when Sarah used to make derogatory remarks about Paul. Now it was Sarah Barnes who temporarily wrecked the plans both of Tony and myself. She also nearly wrecked Paul King. The way it happened was this.

Stratford came across with an even more tempting offer, a big chance, three chances, in fact, Orlando, Mercutio and Hamlet. And they wanted a quick answer, being fed up with frigging around, and I didn't blame them.

Paul had got a one-room flat of his own, now, thank God, off Baker Street. Tony came on the blower to me within an hour of the Stratford offer. He sounded understandably irritated. Ten percent of eighty pounds a week isn't rich gravy, not compared with fat gravy from the film offers. We agreed to meet Paul for drinks at the Ritz bar that morning.

It was the crunch all right. Paul's conceit was smoldering heavily, fanned by the breeze from the Avon. But I think that after the second drink we had swung him away from Stratford. At the start, we were all united on one thing.

Stuff called money. Tony wanted big film money for Paul, Paul wanted big money for Paul, I wanted big money for Paul. Money starts by whispering in the Ritz, or any big hotel where the good things of life can be had for it. After the second drink, it shouts.

Then Sarah Barnes had to go and appear with her own agent. Tall and dark, but no longer gawky. She'd filled out and looked pretty good to me. Except that her eyes snapped as she came up to our table. I felt in my bones it boded no good. But at the first exchange, I thought I was wrong, I thought it boded considerable good.

"Darling Paul! What a lovely surprise!" she cried, though with a touch of the old tinny in her voice, and kissed him. "Both of us being wooed by the Royal Shakespeare Company—two old Durrington hacks, who'd have thought it?"

"You too?" asked Paul, and by golly you couldn't say the surprised tone was exactly complimentary. "Well, well," he added, and then again, "well, well."

It was at this point that I thought that the idea of his old enemy Sarah going to Stratford with him just about clinched the victory in our favor. So it might have done, it she'd left it at that.

"Orlando, Mercutio, and Hamlet!" she gushed. "Darling, what a wonderful offer! And all these film offers!"

"Who told you the details?" asked Paul coldly. She snapped her eyelashes at him again.

"What details, darling?"

"About Stratford," he said abruptly.

"One does have one's spies, one likes to know who one will be acting with, doesn't one? Orlando, Mercutio—Hamlet," she cooed. "But are you wise, Paul darling?"

"Wise?"

I think she knew what she was doing. I think she was genuinely upset at the idea of acting with him again, trying to put him off.

"Think of all the lovely lolly from films, darling—and think of all the actors who have been ruined, but ruined, by trying to play *Hamlet,* darling! You really *must* think deeply, Paul. Orlando and Mercutio—yes, but Hamlet, darling?"

I still think she was trying to put him off, but there are times when I think she was needling him. Not with the idea of getting him to Stratford, far from it, but just to annoy him, because she couldn't resist it.

"I would say I have as much chance of playing Hamlet reasonably well as most people," Paul said softly.

Tony Banks was slowly waking up to the danger, but very slowly. He said, "Of course he has, Sarah."

"Darling Tony, Paul isn't *most* people, is he? Or is he?"

I listened to it all with a much faster growing dismay than Tony. I suddenly realized that the tide of victory had swung the other way. The watershed had been reached, Paul had begun to believe his own handouts, any suggestion that he, Paul King, couldn't do Hamlet was an insult and a challenge. Bad at any time, almost fatal coming from Sarah Barnes. With drooping heart, I heard her plunge still further, knee deep in it, drunk with pleasure because she was annoying him.

"Of course, if you *can* get away with it, it'll be fine, absolutely fine, darling!"

"It's not a question of him getting away with it," snapped Tony, now thoroughly alerted. "There's the money angle."

"Well, do think it over carefully, Paul darling," she cried, and whisked off to join her own agent. Paul watched her go with hate-filled eyes. Tony glanced after her, too, looking as if he wished her to drop dead. Even if she had, it would have been too late. We both knew that.

I had a lunch date and had to leave the stricken battlefield.

Tony called to pick me up on the way to the show that evening, and his first words were, "Paul's decided it's his big chance, and as he's acted with Sarah before, they could make a great team."

I paused as I poured out our gins, then added a bit more gin to relieve the shock.

"A great team? He and Sarah? What are they going to carry, knives or strychnine?"

118

"That's what he says," muttered Tony. "Also thinks he mustn't become too commercial, that's what he says. Says it'll be better for me, too, in the long run."

People are always inclined to keep on the sunny side of their motives. The moment they have tripped somebody up they explain how much more comfortable he'll be lying flat on his face, not worrying about his corns any more. Paul was no exception.

"Of course, I'm very fond of Paul," said Tony, which is always a hopeful beginning. When anyone says that you can bet your last dollar something juicy will come up.

"He has been a bit difficult since his success," he went on, and began moaning about the sad lot of agents. It was quite a stretch of tape.

I poured him out another large gin.

"After all, I found *Deeper in the South* for him, and spent £20 giving lunch to that *tiresome* American producer," said Tony. Tony had been friendly with Harry Alvarez. But things move on quickly in show-biz.

"I've seen all the rushes of the film, and he's going to get rave notices for that, too. Joe Gross is thrilled, and he's offering £60,000, rising to £80,000, a film for the next three years. What the hell does Paul think he is doing, opting out for eighty a week, and a three-year contract at Stratford?"

I could see that three years of meager commission for Tony had stuck in his mind, and probably his gullet, too.

"Still, Joe Gross is an old friend of mine. We've fixed it up between us. It's on a year-to-year basis, and Joe has a lien on Paul's services on a one-film basis—gentlemen's agreement on the rest."

"In that case," I said, "why worry? After all, Joe could come up with a better offer if this first film hits the jackpot."

Tony was thinking that one out, too. The idea was germinating. He was looking at the end of his cigar in a contemplative way.

"Fortunately, they are doing *As You Like It* and *Romeo* first. He will be good in those."

"He will be good as Mercutio and Orlando," I agreed,

voicing his unspoken thoughts. I knew what he was thinking. If Paul got good notices for the first two productions,
that was the moment to strike in the film world, while the
iron was hot. Before he took the dreaded Hamlet jump.

"Play it by ear," I said comfortingly, because I am everybody's friend.

Paul filled in some of the months, till Stratford opened,
finishing the film for Joe, doing bits and pieces of reshoot-
ing and recording the dialogue, post syncing as they call
it. In the end Joe was delighted with the film.

"Now, there's a boy who has everything. I've got a hunch
about him. This little film we've made, nothing much, but
he's going to lift it out of the rut. It's not often I get a real
stroke of luck. He's a nice boy."

The bloom was still on the grapes of the contracts.

13

I thought of taking Stella Fenton to the opening of the
Stratford season. It was a good idea for her to be seen around.
As it happened, neither of us could go, and it was a month
or so before I managed to get down. That's how it is with
publicity, things blow up, films, first nights, and you have
to be on the spot. It's like being in the balloon business, one
minute everything is very large and the next you've got nothing but a small piece of shriveled rubber. But while the
balloons are large and still floating, you have to be around.
It was early May when I finally went there. Stratford-on-
Avon is pleasant at that time of year. Even the swans seem
to be relaxing before their summer peak performances.
Makes you feel good to sit on the benches outside the Dirty
Duck pub, watching the river, and the young spear carriers
hamming it up on the wooden benches outside the pub.

The shorter their parts, the longer their hair, the higher their boots and the thicker their sweaters.

Shirley had asked me to lunch, and as I didn't want to be too early, I sat by the river, relaxing, amused by the spear carriers. Some of them even carried small volumes of the play currently in rehearsal. Nothing like giving a whiff of local color to the passing carriage trade. I looked at them and remembered Paul and that it was only a couple of years or so since he, too, could have looked like that. He'd had it very easy.

At midday, I drove over to Paul's married quarter, outside the town. And when I say "married quarter" I mean just that, because it's like being on the North West Frontier, under Imperialism, at Stratford—officer class stars, N.C.O. bit players, and spear carrier other ranks.

Paul's quarter was part of a country house. I walked across the stable yard and climbed some steep stairs, and found myself in a sort of chauffeur's flat. Nice when you got there. Lovely to see Shirley, of course, even though she poured out cheap sherry. Paul didn't waste dough on gin. I could see the river and the gray spire of Stratford church.

"How's it all going?" I said, settling down on the settee and smiling the good old Charlie smile.

"Everyone is being so difficult," said Shirley, worried and anxious. I admit I gave an inward groan.

This was where I came in, a week ago, a month ago, a year ago, two years ago. Whenever I came in, it was poor, bloody, self-pitying Paul. These one-man women can be trying, unless you're the one-man. If you are, all fine and dandy. If not, then dear God, you've got to be prepared to sweat it out in whatever cause you have in sight. And when I say sweat, I don't mean just get a little moist.

If anyone was being difficult, it was Paul. The drums had been beating and I'd heard a bit of gossip. I don't always believe it, but I take note of it. In my business you have to.

"Paul says Stratford is like a goldfish bowl," droned Shirley. "But then, when you are as talented as Paul, you do get a lot of jealousy."

"Surely Paul was happy about his notices for Orlando?"

"Oh, yes. But it's very upsetting, all this jealousy."

I could imagine some bit players who had been putting their very souls into "What ho, within there," or "He did, my Lord," feeling narked when Paul, who had never carried a spear in his life, was brought down on the strength of a few West End notices and given three plum parts.

"I'm not saying Paul isn't temperamental, he *is.*"

She looked at me, and I could see that things weren't running as sweetly as the Avon. Was it the beginning of the end? I felt a sudden leap of pleasure.

"When you have a great talent," she went on, "people should expect this. So must I," she said determinedly.

"He got very good notices for Orlando," I insisted, keeping the whole thing on a cheerful level.

"Paul is a dedicated actor, utterly dedicated." Shirley was at it again. I sighed. "Do you think Tony is commercial?"

I could hardly believe my ears. When agents aren't commercial, that will be the day.

"Still, as Paul says, Tony was never much of an actor. He doesn't understand things as Paul does," said Shirley.

I wondered. I remembered Tony's expression: "Paul will be okay as Orlando and Mercutio." No mention of Hamlet. Ex-actors aren't so easily fooled.

I watched Shirley go through into the bedroom, saw her leaning across the cot to waken Jane. A simple action, full of tenderness, something Shirley didn't receive herself.

After lunch, I left. I wasn't going to stay to see Paul come home to the possession of Shirley, to watch his dedicated artist performance, see his dissatisfied expression. I had no feeling for turning knives in wounds. Even a little surface salt can be painful.

I was walking down towards the Shakespeare Hotel, where I was staying, when I saw Vic Jones meandering vaguely along.

"Hello, hello," I called out. "What are *you* doing here?"

A bit too hearty, a bit too surprised to see him, but you can't always get impromptu performances right.

"Got a few walk-ons—oldest spear carrier in the business. I think Sarah fixed it."

"Come and have a drink."

I jerked my head towards the hotel. He looked a bit nonplussed. Other Ranks don't mix in Officer Class bars. It is not that the officers don't like the men. Couldn't find a better bunch of chaps anywhere—anyone who has fought his way with them through *Henry V* will tell you they're a good mob. Best in the world. But discipline is discipline.

Vic hesitated for a second and then he followed me into the hotel bar. We sat down and I ordered drinks. It was one of those talks. Jerky. Chat about the old days. Chat about Sarah Barnes. Chat about Paul. Chat about Vic's father, who was very ill up in Newcastle, and how Vic thought perhaps he ought to pull out of Stratford and go north. Then, back to Paul King.

"Hasn't changed, has he?" said Vic. "He's got a heavy load of genius to carry around. Dead lucky, he's been." Not bitter. Just a statement of fact. "Quite the Golden Boy. Heard about *Hamlet?*"

He sipped his drink.

"I know Ferrini's directing."

"Sort of Borgia orgy, it's going to be. Sets like a cross between St. Mark's, Venice, and the Sistine Chapel, Rome. Still, Paul's got a good leg for tights."

His expression was not malicious, just amused. He could see I wasn't going to be drawn about Paul, and switched to me. "You glad you gave up the business?"

"Not sorry. There are compensations."

"Tricky stuff, publicity. Like being at the Court of Louis XV—on the staircase. You never know whether you're on the way in, or on the way out."

I changed the subject.

"Doing anything in *Hamlet?*"

"Understudying George Blane's gravedigger."

"Let's hope for the best, then."

We knew what that meant. We both knew that George liked his booze. That's how it is, a couple of pints after thin houses in Rep turns into a half bottle of the hard stuff when success smiles. The Royal Shakespeare is the Royal Shakespeare, and *Hamlet* is *Hamlet,* and the gravedigger is an okay part, provided he doesn't dig his own grave.

"Good actor, George," said Vic. He was a man who could never understand Iago, the false friend.

We chatted on and then I watched him go out of the hotel, the kind of man you don't often meet, someone who makes you feel that everyone isn't a bastard.

I went upstairs and my phone rang. Paul on the line. Would I please come round after the show without fail. Kind of eighteenth-century lord sending for his attorney. I went round. He was still in his make-up with his dresser buzzing round.

"I was disappointed you haven't been down before, to see me as Orlando," he said abruptly.

Superficially, he had a point. Useless to tell him you don't need to taste tapioca in order to advertise the product.

"Terribly disappointed myself, Paul. Got tied up with a lot of small stuff. Chicken feed, but necessary, when you're struggling."

I shrugged hopelessly. Poor bloody peasant, trying to hack a living out of the recalcitrant soil. He was slightly mollified.

"You realize that the first night of *Romeo* is the same week as the film opens?" he said sulkily. "I do feel that you haven't been making enough of an effort lately."

I put on the good old Charlie, but slightly crestfallen friend look. Dead easy to an actor.

"I was holding my fire until the play and film opened. I've brought some of the stills from the film down for you to okay." Underling stuff.

"Joe ran the film through for me this week," I added brightly.

"How did you like it?"

"Marvelous! It made me feel terribly proud to think we started together. Terribly proud. I feel I'm helping to create something worthwhile," I added simply. Amazing how they fall for that guff. As I began to outline my publicity campaign, photographs, interviews, contacts I had made, I watched the ballon of his ego starting to fill nicely.

He nodded to me, politely dismissing. The audience was over. I went out into the passage and walked towards the back of the stage and stood there in the darkness looking at the empty auditorium. Was it Chekhov who said, "All I know is, backstage, the ballerinas stink like horses"?

I turned and made my way down towards the stage door. Alas, no smell of horses. Backstage, Stratford didn't smell like other theatres. It still had a clean, hospital smell. Almost too clean for a theatre, in my view, but I'm old fashioned.

The evening was cold, and I walked along by the river, forgetting Paul's humiliating words in front of the dresser, savoring Shirley's words about tension in the marriage. Something was beginning to work at last.

Stella came down to the first night with me, looking very fancy. Italian silk two-piece, and a bit of mink for throwing about. That red hair looked splendid. She was being very nice to me, because most people are nice to me on the way up, and Stella was a girl with her eye on the top rung.

"Isn't this *fun?*" she said, smiling half at me and half at a passing photographer.

She spoke too soon. I caught sight of a hanging cigarette and Edith hove in view, coughing as usual. There was nothing wrong with her lungs, Paul had told me. She was just one of nature's coughers. Bit chesty, that's all.

"Hello," she croaked, "I managed to get a lift down."

Edith made this sound like a reproach. No one should set off without making sure Edith had transport.

"Paul doesn't look at all well," she wheezed into my ear. "Shouldn't be surprised if he had a cold."

She stared at me ominously.

"It's that child—always picking up something, and passing it on. Hope the show's going to be all right tonight."

She gave a baleful look in the direction of the auditorium, and tottered off to find her seat.

"Who is that extraordinary woman?" said Stella, as Edith's ashy figure disappeared.

"Paul's mother."

"I don't believe it. She looks more like Dracula's aunt."

Stella's eyes were darting this way and that. Definitely beady. A girl who didn't miss a trick.

"Do you see who that is?" I half turned. "It's Gregory Konzakis, the film director."

I looked again. It was. Very glossy, like a cheerful, well-fed shark who used a good brand of toothpaste.

Konzakis was supposed to be Greek. A fashionable nationality, full of sun and sea, and joy of living, but Konzakis looked as if he filed his teeth. His real name was Knopmuss and he'd started with Joe Gross as a clapper boy at Elstree.

"I wonder why Konzakis is here," said Stella reflectively, tossing her red hair, because you never know, do you? Film directors sometimes discover girls at first nights.

"Perhaps he's mad about the Bard. He won't have to pay for the film rights," I said acidly.

Nobody need have worried about Paul's Mercutio. I was surprised. I must reluctantly admit that he brought a flashy dash and edge to the character.

There was a party after the show. People drifting about seeing if there was anyone useful around. Just the kind of thing for Stella. She dived straight in, making her way deviously toward Konzakis, a girl you didn't have to coach.

I'd been playing dumb bunnies with Stella. I'd a pretty shrewd idea why Konzakis was swimming in these waters. It had been in the paper that he was going to do a film about Rupert Brooke. Should be a cinch with lush pre-1914 settings, end-of-the-garden-party-into-the-waste-of-war stuff. Whoever got the part of Rupert Brooke had got it made. Paul looked right. He was a Young Apollo, golden haired.

Poor old Joe Gross, the deep-sea fishermen were after his inshore catch. And the bait was good. An historical national hero, a background of culture, a sensitive director (so the Press said), a big budget and a chance of world fame. I looked across the room. Stella, Konzakis, and Paul were all standing together. I wondered whether they were singing the same song. I needn't have wondered.

Tony came in to see me two days later.

"I've been talking to Joe," he said, without preamble. He'd been giving Joe lunch on the old pals basis.

Boiled down, what his story amounted to was that he'd pointed out to Joe Gross that surely he wouldn't think of wrecking a promising career like Paul's, and jeopardizing the future of Paul's wife and Paul's child. Joe pointed out that he had a future, too, and what was more, he was hanging on to it.

So far, £10 on lunch wasted, Joe and Tony both took their contracts to solicitors.

Paul was rehearsing Hamlet now, and far too busy to discuss money, though he did find time to phone Tony and tell him to ask for £100,000.

Tony came to see me. What about a little publicity on the subject? Why not? I was all for it. The balloon was going up nicely.

Next day, we made all the evenings with pictures of Paul, and captions saying, "Stratford Actor to Play Poet?" The boys who put in the query were no dopes.

Meanwhile down on the Avon, as in London, small print was being read. Maybe some spears would be thrown for a change. But they weren't, three-year contract or not. Nothing happened. Not even a swan's feather was ruffled. After all, there were other actors, and Stratford was, as Paul had said, a world stage. And if he wanted to leave it for the Odeon that was up to him. Contract or no contract. Let him go, they said, let him go.

Joe was a different kettle of fish. He was a fighter. He wasn't giving up and, anyway, he wasn't a world stage.

Big money is like a charge of dynamite. It brings out the real seams in the personality. It amused me to watch the change in relationship between Paul and Tony. He became

Paul's zombie, trotting backwards and forwards with offers, and prospectively netting a share of the gross as well as a fee from Konzakis. Licking his lips.

With the offer tucked in his pocket, Tony gave Joe another meal—dinner at the Savoy Grill, this time. Tony threw the lot at him—caviar, turtle soup with sherry, some wretched game bird flown from abroad, savory, champagne, brandy, cigars.

Joe, a second-generation Jewish refugee, had always seen Tony as the English gentleman Tony had so often played. I could have told him something—the higher the stakes, the thinner on the ground gentlemen get, and the worst kind of agreements are gentlemen's agreements. They presuppose the widespread existence of gentlemen in the twentieth century.

Joe couldn't match the offer.

When contracts were again consulted, Joe's case didn't look so cast iron. What is more, the lawyers said it would be expensive to sue, and when a lawyer says expensive, he means it.

Joe gave up. Tony phoned me the news, just in time for the morning papers.

"Paul King to Play Poet." "£100,000 role for Ex-Rep Actor." All that old routine. I never did believe in type casting. When it came to it, only the Jew had behaved like a gentleman.

"It was absurd of Joe," said Tony, "to think he could hang on to Paul. Paul is a big name." The wonderful perfume of real money hung in the air. "Joe's small time. I like Joe, but he's small."

And getting smaller every day.

"Now with Konzakis, Paul is on sure ground, he's a splendid director."

"Artistic, too," I said, but Tony didn't smile.

"Exactly."

"It's not," I said sincerely, "as if Paul had sold out to commerce."

"We've all got to do our best for Paul's career, that's the important thing."

I quoted a piece I'd had to learn at school, putting the whole thing on an arty level: "We passed Rupert's island at sunset . . . every color had come into the sea and sky . . . it seemed that the island must be ever shining with his glory that we buried there." I have my cultured moments.

"I wonder if they've seen that bit for the script," Tony said.

"Should come over well in color, if you get the weather."

Tony looked at me, but I had on my good old Charlie face. You can't fault me when I'm on form.

"What about your publicity arrangements with Joe?"

"I've been doing Paul just for this last film. Konzakis will have his own boys." I wasn't pushing myself. "But, of course, if I can do anything extra for Paul, I will." As he said, we all had to do our best for Paul.

"I've been talking to Paul about that. He feels that you *know* him. You've got a pretty good idea about the right kind of stuff for him, and he wants you to carry on. Paul feels he needs someone who understands his image."

Good dog Spot was being thrown a bone. Besides, good dog Spot could be brought to heel.

"I could handle things on a more *personal* basis," I agreed modestly.

We didn't mention Joe again. Didn't strew a single flower.

I went to see the Konzakis boys the following day and started to get going. There was plenty to do, what with the advance stuff for the film and bits of personal stuff for Paul. Rep to Riches makes a good story, like winning the pools.

He was now all set to pop the crown of Hamlet, Prince of Denmark, on his golden locks.

Vic Jones had said Ferrini saw Hamlet as a Renaissance prince. But the kind of sets which had been dreamed up looked to me more like an arrangement for a conference in Julius Caesar's time. Ferrini's ancestors must have worked at the Roman games, and even then the Colosseum would have been pushed for space.

When the ghost himself remarked, "Oh, horrible, most horrible," he spoke the play's epitaph in advance.

I was sitting in the circle and didn't see anyone I knew, not even Shirley. I didn't care about Paul, but I did care for her humiliation. Hamlet is like Becher's Brook, at the Grand National; you either sail over, hooves clear water, or go straight in. I could tell from the first scene that Paul was going in, head first.

While Stratford has ways of flying scenery, moving it off mechanically sideways, and throwing clouds on cycloramas, it is usually supposed that these don't have to be done all at one and at the same time. Ferrini apparently thought they should. One critic described the play as The Last Days of Elsinore.

Marble pillars tottered. The players had to weave their way through Renaissance death traps. If disaster, like justice, must be seen to be done, it was seen that night, all right. At least when you get the smoke of battle in the Histories, it does fuzz up the effects a bit. The clear light of the Renaissance day was a mistake.

As I watched Paul floundering, it was like double vision. I minded because his success was my weapon, which would separate him from Shirley. Failure would bring her closer than ever to his side, and yet I had a mean feeling of pleasure at the idea he could fail, and fail so dismally.

His failure didn't involve Sarah Barnes. She wasn't playing Ophelia. That was something, and at first I thought that no one I liked was involved in the shipwreck.

I was wrong about that, because George Blane for once had misjudged his alcoholic capacity, and Vic was playing the gravedigger, his big chance. That was a joke, he wasn't playing it, he was speaking it. He was boring, dull and sentencious. This wasn't Shakespeare's gravedigger, just an undertaker out of Dickens. For once I was glad to hear the words: "Take up the bodies," and see the curtain come down.

The corpse of the play had been underground the whole evening.

A few late stragglers were making their way out of the Stage Door as I went in. As I turned toward the staircase,

I ran into Tony. He wasn't looking as glossy as usual, needless to say.

"How is he?"

"It wasn't his fault, it was all due to the contract rows." If that was his story for Konzakis, he might as well get it right straight away. "And what about that idiotic scenery?" he said. "I shouldn't go and see him now," Tony added ominously.

"Okay. Shall I ring the notices through tomorrow? I could go back to London tonight."

I knew the papers didn't catch the crits for the early editions.

"I shouldn't bother," said Tony glumly.

I went on down the corridor.

"Where are you going?"

"I might have a word with Vic Jones."

"He didn't help."

I shrugged my shoulders. When disaster strikes, everyone gets the blame. I pushed open the door of the dressing room. Vic was lying with his head in his arms. He was alone. The harsh lights of the make-up tables lit the back of his head. Over the mirror hung the good luck telegrams.

What can you do about complete humiliation? Nothing to say, nothing at all. I walked quietly out, and went back to my hotel.

The next day was sunny. I was in two minds about telephoning Shirley. It might be awkward. Especially if Paul was there. He wasn't likely to be in a good mood.

I was strolling down towards the river when I ran straight into him. He was walking up that hill which leads along the side of New Place gardens, and looked a lot more like Hamlet this morning than he had done the previous night.

"Bloody shambles last night," he said indignantly. "Absolute bloody, flaming shambles, that's what it was."

"Oh, I don't know," I said. "They had a bit of bother with the sets, but it'll shake down."

"My notices won't."

"Have you read them?"

"No, and I don't intend to read them. It won't make a blind bit of difference. Every bloody thing was wrong, including your old friend Vic making a stinking monkey of the gravedigging scene. George was drunk as a newt. Fancy playing with Vic, that bit of old second-hand Rep! I ask you! You'd think they'd get better stand-ins than that. Afterwards I asked him what the hell he thought he was doing, and all he said, standing in the wings like a bloody dummy, was 'My father is dead,' and burst out crying. Should have cried about the performance. That would have been more to the point."

Now I knew what had happened. I saw quite clearly. In his mind's eye, Vic had been digging his own father's grave. The Gravediggers are described as clowns in my Shakespeare. Laugh, clown, laugh. Poor Clown, he hadn't got much to laugh about.

It wasn't my day. Walking up the street I met Edith. She was coming out of the Arden, dropping ash on the roses.

"Going back to London?"

She looked at me through her smoke screen. It was one of those moments when one's head is too full of other things to think of an excuse.

I gave in, and I knew I was in for a couple of hours of smoky gloom. She was soon off on her usual tack. How Paul's career had been endangered by Shirley and by Jane. How she herself wasn't capable of working any more, and I could well see, with the smell of large sums of money in the offing, that her health naturally wouldn't last out. How she didn't think that Shirley could possibly give Paul the background when he needed it as an important film star. I wanted to ask "Who says film stars are important?" but kept my trap shut, because I know which side my press cuttings are buttered.

Edith had thought of an entirely new slant on the Hamlet disaster. It turned out to be Shirley's fault for encouraging Paul to come down to Stratford in the first place. Nice old girl, Edith, she had all the angles, though mind you, if she was talking to Paul about Shirley in this vein she was doing me a bit of good. It's like telling the peasants they are oppressed—they up and burn down the farm if you keep on at it long enough. Bowling along the Oxford Road with Edith was like taking a long cruise with Jeremiah. Sack cloth and ashes. You couldn't call her dress sack cloth, but the floor of the car was covered in ash, and ragged butts hung out of the ash tray. We got to Cromwell Road, and I turned towards Earls Court.

"I've moved. I'm living in Maida Vale," she said, happy for the first time, because it was in the opposite direction. Reproachful, too, implying I should have realized. I got lost and ended up near the Zoo.

"This isn't the way the bus comes," she pointed out.

I didn't reply. I found her house and dumped her. She got out, carrying a large bunch of flowers, two lettuces, and some spring onions from Shirley's garden. No point in going to the country if you don't pick up unconsidered trifles.

Konzakis was a sharp operator in the publicity field. After the tragedy of the Lord Hamlet they soft pedaled Paul. Like an orchestra leader, he was giving Paul a couple of bars' rest. The public has a short memory. Besides, he realized that publicity, like the cream in Irish coffee, can be overdone. Too much, and it sickens the palate.

He sent for me. He had a large desk, and plenty of carpet for minions to walk over before they reached the presence.

His film company had a big house in Mayfair. Not even a brass plate on the door. Ducal stuff. Gives the investors confidence if they feel the background is sound. He didn't look up when I went into his office. Just went on reading an important paper and then spoke to someone on the intercom. Nothing like putting the peasants in their place. When he'd finished giving this performance, he turned to me and switched on a faint flicker of interest.

"Ah, Mr. Maither, you've seen my publicity boys?" He had one of those mid-Atlantic voices, acquired on his way up. "You've done a good job on Paul so far."

I looked grateful and reassured.

"A good jarb," he repeated. A bit nearer New York, the voice was now.

"Now this film is going to be big, and we don't want any slip-ups. I'll hire you to handle the personal angle. I want you to play along with my boys, work in with them, and I don't want trouble. I don't want any of the corny low-level stuff. I don't want any small time pictures of Paul wearing the newest line in shirts." I could hear he'd got the same cuttings agency as I had. "You can do better than that. And lately, you *have* been doing better." Glossy and sharp, he looked like a steak knife with a serrated edge. But the terms he offered were good.

"I hire you on a monthly basis. Okay?" People like to use the word "hire." Puts the hands in their place.

"Okay," I said humbly.

"We don't want any domestic stuff—*no* photographs of wife and child, we're soft pedaling them. Nothing cozy. Understand? I've paid a lot of money for Paul. This is going to be a tragic motion picture. It's about a doomed poet."

Fortunately, he didn't insist on telling me the story.

"I don't want Paul to go about smiling—it spoils the image."

He let his pearls sink in.

"I've okayed the script, and we shall start shooting as soon as Paul gets rid of Stratford."

The Bard was in the dress basket. The band wagon was ready to move off. I thought of that poem, "The Golden Road To Samarkand," and that line where it says, "Our camels sniff the evening and are glad," glad to be on their way. Chief Camel Konzakis had sniffed the evening and was glad to be on his way.

The Chief Camel growled and grunted again, "I shan't want you on location. I'll have one of my own boys handle the local stuff and keep the clamps down there. I want you to sift the national stuff. We don't want any cheerful romping news pictures leaking out. I'm keeping Paul under wraps until the film is premièred."

He pronounced it "premeered." No one would have thought he'd been born in Acton, England. He turned to his intercom. The audience was at an end. I slid out.

One thing I learnt from the publicity boys in a mews office at the back was that Paul was going to be away some months and Stella had landed herself a small part in the film. She was going on location as a sympathetic nurse at the poet's death bed. A Red Cross nurse. That would annoy her, with one of those veils on, because no one would see her red hair, but the way up is hard.

This news pleased me, considering the look Paul had given her at the party. You never know, I thought.

On the Avon, the season jogged to its end. *Hamlet* never really got off the ground. Paul was unpopular in the Company. Total shipwreck has to be blamed on someone, and he was the most prominent rock in sight. The newspaper stories of the largesse showered on his head didn't help. People are unsympathetic about large sums of money, unless they own them themselves.

The film epic of *Young Apollo* took four months to make. Shirley was on her own, and all she saw of Paul were one or two selected publicity shots, chosen by me, looking handsome in his poet's rig and World War I uniform, against Greek island backgrounds. All the news she got from him were postcards and, occasionally, long distance phone calls.

He said to me before he left, "Look after Shirley. She wants a house in the country. Keep her busy, go house hunting with her. She knows how important this is to me, and that I can't drag her about with me."

The rocket was beginning to think its booster was a dead weight. I always thought it would.

So Shirley and I went house hunting, and in the end we found the perfect house, on the borders of Hampshire and Sussex. Paul agreed by cable, without question or comment.

"He doesn't seem to care where he lives," Shirley said. She seemed puzzled and disappointed.

"I don't think men care as much for their caves as women," I said. "All that matters is that Paul wants you to be happy, and you want his film to have every chance, don't you?"

She was fervent in her agreement. I don't often pat myself on the back but I never played a better "Charles, his friend," than in those months.

"When I think of how far he's gone," she said, "it's like some wonderful, beautiful dream."

The rushes were splendid, and Paul and Tony were basking in the sunshine of contracts and offers which came in on every tide. Our publicity was going well, too. Very prestigey stuff. Nothing common. All on a very high level. *Daily Telegraph,* weekly glossies, a double spread in a color supplement. Very much the tragic poet, with a nice slice of Greek island as a backdrop. They'd got a good shot of a sunset, too. Rupert's island had "come out good, but good," as Konzakis said.

Then one day Konzakis sent for me. I wondered what the disaster was. But I'd guessed incorrectly.

"Great news," he said, and smiled, and I thought if he didn't wear a shark's-skin dinner jacket, he ought to.

"*Apollo's* been chosen for the Royal Film Performance! The Queen is coming herself."

And that indeed was a long way from Acton, London W.11.

We discussed some dignified publicity and then I went round to see King Paul. He'd taken a furnished flat in Arlington House. Handy for the Caprice. It looked like a tart's bedroom in a film set, all padded.

I listened to him jazzing on about his publicity, taking pencil notes of his views about his own image, scribbling away in my little notebook, looking up happily from time to time with my good dog Rover look. Thinking what a great big piece of phonus bolonus he was.

Double think is handy. I was still taking down his pearls of great price, when I heard him say, "The thing I like about you, Charlie, the thing I've always liked about you, is that I always know what you're thinking. We work well together.

Why don't you have lunch with me—Konzakis has called off our date—I'll take you to the Caprice."

Nice bone for good dog Rover. Show him a good time.

Later, we had one of those conferences in Wardour Street where everyone talks in strings of figures, some of which they hope will drift their way. It was a conference about the "premeering" of *Apollo* in New York. We were all talking like that now, getting nearer to Manhattan in our speech every minute. Most of the men there, except a couple of the top boys, were English, but from the way they talked you'd have thought they had all been born anywhere between Albuquerque, New Mexico, and the Bronx. We were talking a lot about flying to the Coast, too. All on a very high level, it was. Big executive stuff.

When the conference broke up into little groups, I went out. It had been mooted that I should go along with Paul to New York. Sort of cross between a personal handout man and a nanny, as far as I could see. What they really wanted was a buffer between the news men and Paul. Keeping up the prestige.

I wasn't keen. I couldn't just drop my business like that, I had got other projects. The front boys thought my diffidence due to the fact that I wanted to stick them for an extra fee. They didn't mind that. They expected it, it was what they would have done themselves.

Afterwards, as I was walking down Wardour Street, I saw towering above me Paul's tragic doomed poet, and very nice, too. It gave me satisfaction to see him posturing there as if I'd been some kind of sorcerer who had changed him from a man into a paper image.

The film world is a small place and the next minute I ran into Joe Gross. He was standing on the corner of the street, looking up at the poster of Paul.

I waved a greeting. I hadn't fallen foul of Joe, you have to keep in with everyone. He still looked up at the poster with his sad eyes.

"In the big time, now?" he asked.

"Not me. I'm just fringe scum."

"That applies to a lot of us."

"I was sorry you lost out," I said, "but there was nothing I could do."

"I know that. That's motion picture business for you."

He gave me one of his mock Jewish gestures, and a bitter little smile.

"When I'm dealing with crooks, I like a good honest crook. You know where you are, and keep your wallet pocket buttoned. It's this highminded stuff that really gets me. 'No one has the *right* to keep an actor back from fulfilling his artistic destiny.' I hate arty crap. Hear the boy's really made good."

I nodded.

"Always knew it. I hear from the boys that Paul thinks I'm a sharp character, talking him into such a moldy contract in the first place. You heard that?"

"Several versions are about."

"People like to give themselves a good character. Makes them feel better. Once in a while they could do themselves a favor, and take a good look at themselves."

He shrugged his shoulders, and we parted with an offhand, "See-you."

We were going in opposite directions, anyway. I watched him going down the street. A small figure in the pushing crowds, getting still smaller.

I didn't intend to go to the Royal Première; by that time I'd seen the film three times, and although I'm a glutton for punishment, there are limits, even to my endurance. Not to mention the prints or stills I'd been pushing out, and the intimate lunches and dinners for chatting-up purposes. Even if they have clamped down on the old expense account racket, a ten quid lunch pays off if you get a double spread. Besides, I'm well in with Fleet Street and never push out the same story twice.

I'd started to do a bit more work on Stella. I thought it was time. Just a bit here and there, plugging the promising actress bit. And she was photogenic. Ex-Rada student on road to stardom, and I'd managed to get this color shot of her leaning over the dying poet. I'm not sure whether there were any nurses at the poet's death bed, but there were in the film. It made a good page in one of the glossies. Stella was very pleased. She came to see me in my office. To thank me. She was still in the grateful stage.

She sat on the edge of her chair, looking very pretty, if you go for the pussy kind, and said, "I was wondering if you could fix anything for me at the première."

"It's a bit difficult."

I knew what she wanted. Good coverage, curtseying to the Queen.

"It's out of my hands," I said. "Konzakis will choose the reception line."

"He thinks I've got a future."

She looked at me, wide open eyes, red hair thrown back against a yellow dress. Stella went for simple clothes. Nothing too out of line. Stressed her classic profile.

"He's thinking of me for the next film. Isn't it wonderful?" Very wistful and modest.

"In that case, I will have a word with him," I said at once.

"How *sweet* of you, everyone has been so kind. I'm terribly lucky."

Looking at her sitting there, I thought what a finished piece of goods she was. Like something wrapped in polythene in Fortnums.

"Paul's been terribly kind, too, so helpful in my big scene with him. I shouldn't have been able to do anything without him. Nothing at all."

If Paul was being helpful, I wondered what he wanted out of pussy cat. I looked at her more closely, but her whiskers gave nothing away. She went, and nothing was left in my office but a sharp pungent smell. Not surprising, really, that they fix perfume with the guts of a cat.

I watched the première on the telly. She was in the line all right, with the other two ladies in the film. Looking pretty prominent, too, thanks to lots of white fur and some flashy earrings.

We had a charity party at the River Room in the Savoy

after the show. It's one of those places, like the penthouse at the Carlton Tower, used for anything from posh weddings to launching a new floor polisher, or a bed. Adaptable. When I arrived, the room was fairly empty except for a clutch of debs' mums on the Committee. Parrot ladies screaming "my dear" at one another. But it soon filled up.

Flashes were going off, champagne was circulating, I was circulating, making sure that no one important was being left out in the cold.

"Quite a set-up, I only hope it lasts," said a gloomy voice.

I turned, encountered a pall of smoke, and saw Edith, dressed in gray, which matched her face.

You didn't need a death's head at a party if you asked old Edith. She gave a graveyard cough, and a few sparks fell off the end of her cigarette. She already had two burns in her dress.

"Did you like the film?" Not that I cared. She nodded reluctantly.

"It's the next one that counts," she said gloomily. "And what about that showy house Shirley has bought in the country? Take a lot of keeping up. Her idea, of course. She'll always be a drag on him, mark my words. He ought to have married somebody like Stella Fenton. I've told him so."

"Shirley is a very nice girl, why don't you like her?"

I made the formal protest in favor of Shirley, but I put no feeling into the words. Why should I? If Edith was feeding Paul with pro-Stella propaganda, it suited me all right.

Edith looked at me, her eyes closing against the heavy smoke screen which drifted round her.

"Why don't I like her? It's no good an actor being married to a soppy woman."

I could have hit her, because she was right.

"What about when his films fail?" she asked, back to the old happy line of thought.

"I don't think you need worry about that."

"Here today and gone tomorrow is what I always say."

Edith could have said that about her escaped husband.

A festa of flash bulbs told me Paul King had arrived. He was holding court at the other end of the room, surrounded by gossip writers and opinion formers. Beside him Konzakis smiled. Directing operations, fending off the budding starlets, he moved in the throng, accompanied by his personal Public Relations man, Peter Mason, as Al Capone might have moved with his bodyguard.

Peter Mason, Perry to the boys, was a tall old Etonian with a smooth manner, an arts degree, and a good nose for smelling out failure. He could sniff rot well before it set in, and save the firm money.

Perry was good at his job. His bland manner deceived people into thinking he was an upper crust fool, his arts degree gave a gloss to the handouts, and provided Konzakis with the culture he hadn't got. Not that Konzakis paid him £ 5,000 a year for culture. Culture wasn't worth that kind of money. What gave Perry his sticking power was this nose for rot, and sixth sense about who was on the skids.

I couldn't see Shirley, but I could see Stella, flashlighted every now and again, whiskers on the twitch.

Edith was still droning on, but in my job it's easy to look as if you're listening and be thinking of something quite different. The four-eared publicity man should join the two-toed sloth at the Zoo. Suddenly, I saw Perry making his way towards me, giving out a P.R. distress signal. He pulled alongside and with a swift P.R. smile, detached me from Edith's smoke screen.

"Can you take Shirley home?"

"Why?"

"She's tight. Completely plastered."

She was sleepy in the taxi, sunk in a kind of torpor. No one had noticed us going. The party was hotting up, and she wasn't missed. Wives rarely are, not being usually part of the circus.

She lay close to me, as an animal might get close to another for comfort against dangers, and I put my arm round her. It was odd that the first time we had sat like this should

be because she was plastered. It didn't disgust me. I felt
protective and wanted.

When we got to the flat I took the key out of her bag, and
she stood there, swaying against the lintel of the door. She
didn't even look drunk, she looked like someone who had
been given a shot of something against pain. Some pains
aren't cured by shots.

I took her inside, laid her on the settee, and went into
the kitchen to make some coffee. When I came back she
was lying on her face. Her sobs were uncomfortable to hear.
I sat beside her. Her body was shaking uncontrollably as
if she were falling into a fit. Suddenly she drew herself up.
Tears rolled down her cheeks but her eyes were dull and
seemed beyond feeling. I took her hand and waited.

"What's happening to Paul and me?" she asked in a slurred
voice.

People fall into clichés when deeply moved. Unhappiness is not inspiring. I knew quite well what was happening.

"Do you want to talk about it?" I said. I'm sure it was a
line from some play, but it served its purpose.

"We had a row, a terrible row." There are some antibiotics which make you feel lousy before you get better. I had
planned the antibiotics, and now I was watching the effect,
and not liking it. But it was going to be better for her in the
long run. Better for me, too, but that was beside the point.
Like a firm but benevolent doctor, I hardened my heart.

"Drink your coffee," I said.

I watched her. She was sobering up, and sat there in her
white dress, sipping the coffee, desirable and forlorn. She
reminded me of a line from an old Coward play, "It was
all so lovely in the beginning . . ." I could hear Gertrude
Lawrence's voice saying those words on a long player. "Shadow Play," I think the piece was called, and shadow play
was Shirley's marriage. The loveliness of the beginning
had only been in her mind. It had never been in Paul's. Now
the ballast was beginning to be jettisoned.

She began to talk; a foam of words poured out. This hadn't
been the first row, it had been going on for some time. He

didn't care about her any more, he only cared about his career. He never came home. She was just a bore to him. That evening, at the Arlington House flat, she had suddenly told him he was a selfish bastard. She'd locked herself in the spare room and refused to come to the première. She didn't give a bloody damn any more about him or his flaming career. He should be married to a publicity agent, that was all he wanted.

The whole story of the evening came out, piece by piece. She had stayed at the flat, drinking, and then she had tried to sober up, and taken a taxi to the reception. Maybe it was the second or third glass of champagne which had made her feel so funny. She wasn't used to drinking champagne on top of whisky.

She was so unhappy, all those terrible things she had said to Paul that evening. Di-da-di-da. She started to sob again.

"I know it's no good." She looked at me. "But, Charlie— I *still* want him."

The physical threads were still there, attaching her to him. Her words, spoken one day in Durrington, came back like ghostly whispers, "He says hurtful things and then, suddenly, when he sees he's pained me, he is all tenderness—loving and wonderful."

He would say hurtful things tonight, all right. And then? The wave of jealousy must have shown in my face. Something did. She thought I was affected by drink.

"Charlie, dear, are you *yourself* all right? Drink some more coffee!"

"I'm quite all right, thank you," I said coldly. Farcical situation.

We stayed chatting. After a while, she calmed down. Eventually, she went to bed. She thanked me and kissed me gently on the lips. The kind of kiss she could have given to her child.

I heard her undressing in the bedroom. It was like Durrington again. I could imagine her body but this time not next to his, but alone, needing comfort. I poured myself out a whisky and stood looking towards her bedroom door.

The click of a key made me turn, and Paul came in. He looked at me, half contemptuous, half hopeful, maybe.

"Where is she? You put her to bed?"

"She put herself to bed." Good old Charlie wasn't going to walk into that trap. "It was a pity she should get upset just today."

He shook his head angrily and ruffled his hair with his hand. Distraught stuff. Chap at the end of his tether and all that. An easy role.

"You don't know what it's been like! I *must* have a bit of co-operation! I come home, and it's, 'Where have you been?' 'Have you been working?' 'Who have you been seeing?' Possessiveness eating you bloody well up."

"Perhaps she is afraid of losing you?"

He looked complacent. Thinking himself a great loss. Good old him. Outsize jackpot in the pools.

He went over to the drink table, and poured himself out a tonic water. That was another thing that annoyed me about him, he very seldom drank. In the Builders' Arms it had been, "never more than half-a-pint, not before the performance." And nothing afterwards, because he must get his rest. Now it was the small glass of sherry, and one glass of wine. Of course, it gives you an edge if you're the only one not drinking, especially when it comes to contracts, because you never have the dear-old-pals feeling some people get after a couple of doubles. Everybody is not your friend, and when you stay cold sober you can keep the point in mind. Fiery tonic water in hand, he turned towards me.

"You'd think that just tonight she could have behaved herself—the most important night in my whole career!" He was thinking back on the evening. King Paul popping the crown on his golden hair, bowing to the Queen, almost equals, royalty to royalty, then holding court at the Savoy.

"I'm not taking her to New York, and she can get that straight from the beginning. But I want you to come, Charlie."

His tone of voice said, "You're coming, or else." The voice was like a lash made of pound notes. This amused me. Money

144

may talk, but it wasn't money talking to me. Never had, never did. In view of later events I want to make that clear.

"Yes, I see," I said, slowly.

So I played a scene I'd once done on the stage. The bit where some chap walks up and down, cornered, gazing heavily into his whisky and soda, fighting for time. I did it rather well, better than I'd done it on the stage.

"It's a bit difficult, Paul," I said at last. "I mean, I've got my business to consider—you can't just drop everything like that."

"Yes, you can. You can leave it to Jessie."

I gave another heavy shrug and walked up and down again. A bit humiliated now, but not wanting to show my humiliation. All that phoney stuff.

"Of course," he went on, "if you don't want the job with Konzakis—"

Even for him, that was vulgar. Still, it amused me to see how obvious he was getting, and how power and money sort out the heels from the rest.

"Okay, Paul," I said at last. The beaten down bit, now, slightly slumped shoulders, the kind of thing corrupt politicians did in old films. Complete surrender.

"We're leaving next week," he said, briskly. Another audience was at an end.

I was not so much occupied with thoughts of Tony Banks, and what happened to him, when I left the Builders' Arms on my return to Durrington. That came later.

I was thinking of Paul, on the morning after his West End success, the newspapers around him, all praising him, and yet he, for some reason, unaccountably introspective, hesitating, wondering whether he would or would not see a psychiatrist. What were his worries?

Were they the worries of a normal person unduly magnified by his self-absorption? Were they the worries of a man who knew his drunken father had died in a mental home? Was this why he rarely drank himself? Did he won-

*der whether his father became mentally ill because he drank
—or, more sinister, drank because he had insanity in his
blood, and if the latter, what of himself, Paul King?*

*What was he suddenly afraid of, that morning of his stage
success, what shadow clouded his mind, if any? What somber scene was he conjuring up? Was it a scene from the past,
from Accringham, a scene involving poor little Beryl Wilson, who loved him too much, or was it a possible scene
of the future? Was it something he had done, or something
he might do—or both?*

14

It has been remarked that you don't feel a success until you hit New York. Paul King nearly hit New York. He
nearly hit the pavement from a balcony outside a bar thirty floors up. That is the main reason for briefly recording
the visit.

I nearly murdered him in New York. Deliberately, in
cold blood. The build-up was as follows.

Konzakis and Tony arrived in New York in time for the
Young Apollo première. Everyone was there promoting
the product and protecting the investment.

Two days after the rave notices, Tony barged into my
hotel office, banged the door and said, "Do you realize that
Konzakis is offering Paul £150,000 for his next film?"

He sounded irritated about it.

"Nice to get a raise," I said. I was sitting at my typewriter,
bashing out a couple of Press releases for London.

"He won't accept!"

This didn't surprise me.

"Paul said it wasn't enough, and went off to the country
for the weekend. He's getting impossible."

Poor old Tony. He looked white and fraught, and turned on me.

"You certainly handed me a problem when you handed me Paul."

I'd also handed him a lot of commission but I didn't say anything. What's the good?

"Who's he gone with?"

"I think he went with Stella, to stay with some people she knows, near Pound Ridge. So he *says*. Some people near Pound Ridge! If you can believe that, you can believe anything!"

A nice weekend in the country with that red hair flowing against a white frame house, a drive or two amongst the budding silver birches, and dogwood, and the whole thing should be clinched. Once safely tucked up in Paul's bed, I couldn't see Stella vacating the situation.

I was wrong. Paul was very bad tempered when he came back to Manhattan on Monday. You have to call it "Manhattan," to show you've been there.

My office bedroom was next to Paul's sitting room, and I could hear his voice raised in argument with Tony. Tony's replies were a faint muttering. He wasn't saying much. I could tell he was getting nervous about Paul. There is nothing so expendable as an agent. And nothing so disastrous as to show you know you're expendable. After the altercation, Paul flung open my door.

"I've told Tony he's no bloody good. He can get more for me than that! Much more."

We were squeezing the orange till the pips squeaked, if you could liken Konzakis to anything as fragrant as an orange.

Paul had a nice pile of offers on his plate. Everyone offers you food when you're not hungry. My office was thick with scripts, and I'd become a sieve for telephone calls and Paul wanted to hear my honest opinions. Doubtless, this harked back to our days together in Durrington. Rather like being at the same school. He knew he could trust good old Charlie to have his best interests at heart. Too true he could, the bastard. Should he do a play in London? Should he accept the film thing in Hollywood? Would a play on American TV be sensible before he flew home? I remember how we discussed these problems at a bar at the top of a New York building. There was a concrete platform round the bar, with a safety wall. Part of the wall was missing, a matter of a few feet, pending repairs. The gap was bridged with some planks and a warning notice. We paused by the gap, which was hidden from the bar interior by a corner of the building. We were alone and unobserved. Paul was standing watching the great city down below, his profile against the night sky. The stars in the sky were rivaled by the rivers of light leading to Harlem.

"What do you think, Charlie?—Konzakis is offering me half a million dollars."

This was it. Despite the tinge of blasphemy, I suddenly realized that we were standing on an exceedingly high mountain, and all the cities of the world were down below, lighted up and offering contracts. It was a pleasant prospect for him, the cities of the plain coming across, offering tribute.

"I think it would be a mistake to go back to the theatre—just at this moment. The theatre is something you can do any time, Paul."

I like to think that the voice of the tempter was soft, pleasant and reasonable to him. He was drinking tomato juice. Thick, disgusting looking stuff. He looked into his glass.

"It's a lot of money—a lot of money."

He looked very serious and sincere when he said this. As I said before, money is a very serious and sincere subject. And I was a very serious and sincere friend. If Paul had reached the apex of his career on the very high mountain, I thought I could see the descent to the plains.

"Besides," I went on, speaking in my low, good old Charlie voice, "no one is going to give you a pension. If you accept, what does Konzakis propose?" I asked.

"He's been talking about following up Brooke with Shelley."

If Paul was going to work himself through the Oxford

Book of English Verse, he'd got it made, he could play Tenny-
son at eighty with a gray beard. But I was still looking reflective about Paul's problems.

I said, "Very dramatic story, Shelley, the two wives, and,
of course, it's got modern connotations."

Good word connotations, it covers a multitude of rub-
bish.

"You mean the sex angles?"

"That, and the atheistic thing."

"I'd forgotten that."

He was still looking indecisive. He lifted up his head,
his fair hair lit from behind like an aureole. Very noble he
looked, with that reflective expression, the depths in the
eyes, and the long column of his neck. He only needed a
backing of Chopin. No one would have dreamed he was
mulling over money.

"What do you honestly think, Charlie? You know what
it is with acting, you can easily make the wrong move."

"Only too well."

"After all, it's easy to settle for the big money, and find
you have no career."

"I can see all that," I said, "but once you've got a name,
like yours, and all that money, you're in control."

He liked that bit, "in control," it sounded dominating.

"That's true."

He remained quiet for a while, reflecting deeply about
his favorite subject, himself.

"Yes, I should be in control," he agreed.

He gazed out over the rich city, the tall man-made tow-
ers, the swift moving cars, like mechanical beetles. He was
on top of the world all right.

From far below, came the scream of police sirens. I
looked over the wall, down below into the distant streets,
noting how one stream of cars wavered to let the police
cars go by.

"There they are," I said, disinterestedly, and pointed
below.

Paul King obediently approached the safety wall, except
that where he was standing, there was no safety wall, only

the planks across the gap. He leant cautiously over the top plank, then drew back hurriedly, and swung round, one hand before his eyes.

He said he felt giddy, and stood swaying slightly. I felt giddy, too, but not because of the height.

As he stood there, virtually defenseless, I placed a hand on his shoulder. He thought I had done so to steady him.

It may be thought that before you kill a man you hate, thrust him to his death thirty floors below, you feel a sudden wave of emotion, a surge of excitement, of impending triumph, and a rapid beating of the heart; an atavistic exultation based upon a mixture of blood lust and the thought of slaughtering your enemy.

I am able to state that such is not always the case. The response to the opportunity can be almost automatic.

I felt no emotion. It was as though somebody else had his hand on Paul King's shoulder and I was a mere spectator, uninvolved personally and indifferent to the dictates of law, order and civilization.

Good old Charlie watched almost uninterestedly as Charles Maither moved his hand to Paul King's shoulder.

Nothing came of it. I did not thrust him to death thirty floors below. I pushed him to safety.

I still do not know if this was only because a door leading into the bar suddenly opened, and there was a blare of music and the sound of voices, as a man and woman came out.

I had lunch with Tony a couple of days later. I forget the name of the restaurant. New York has become a blur to me, a place of expensive restaurants, lifts with piped music, rooms with high temperatures, and drinks with ice. Tony had soon cottoned on to the best places to eat in New York. He had that instinctive feeling for small snobberies in other people's countries, just as he had in his own. Some people have a nose for these things.

"What do you think about the script?" he asked.

"It's good."

It was good—in parts. It's difficult to recreate a national

figure. I knew they had got away with it with Rupert Brooke, but the Great War was still in people's minds and memories. The death of Rupert Brooke is linked with the death of a civilization, and the slaughter of the flower of Europe's youth. You'd only got to end with a shot of poppies growing in those flat depressing fields in Flanders, and the audience got the message. Their grandfathers had fought there.

You just had to quote:

> . . .and that unhoped serene,
> That men call age; and those who would have been
> Their sons, they gave, their immortality . . .

It was easy with Brooke. The audience supplied the emotion. Shelley was a different problem. A good poet, but a heel to deal with. One trouble with period stuff is that the script writer easily falls into pish-tushery, while the camera pans about on link boys running with flaming torches, and ladies' bosoms bulging out of Empire dresses. There are a lot of pitfalls in period, and this time the scriptwriter seemed to have fallen into most of them.

"You liked it, really liked it?"

"You can't go wrong with the Regency, can you?" I said evasively. "Who is Konzakis thinking of for the two wives, Harriet Westbrook and Mary Shelley?"

"He's getting Stella for Harriet."

As she drowns herself in the first reel, Konzakis wasn't taking a big risk, but she was making progress. I hadn't seen too much of her since our arrival in New York. Konzakis' American boys had taken her over, but judging by the cuttings, she was doing all right.

"She'll make a good Harriet," I said, "that red hair should look good streaming in the Serpentine."

Harriet Westbrook had been blond, but sometimes one must use a little license. Tony looked at me, his large eyes as troubled as Paul's had been.

"The thing is, Paul hasn't signed up yet."

I could see he had reason for looking troubled. Ten per cent of half a million dollars is worth having.

"I think he'll sign," I said.

"With me, too?"

I looked reassuring, and made a comforting noise.

"I've got no *guarantee* he won't leave me, Charlie."

It is hard being a success boy, and to make sure of your seat on the bandwagon you have to fasten your seat belt with one hand and take tranquilizers with the other.

"I've heard rumors," Tony went on, "I want you to treat this as confidential."

He put on a heavy business face, which didn't suit him. I reassured him about my discretion.

"Some of the things he's been saying about me—"

What he meant was "some of the things he's been shouting at me." I'd heard the tone of voice through the wall. Humiliation is hard to take, but if you help to make a monster, you have to risk feeling its teeth. I said, "It wouldn't be the end of the world if he does leave you. There are other actors, and you're a very well known agent now."

"He means a lot to me."

I felt sorry for the poor sod. I could see it wasn't only the money he minded about. He was attaching a superstitious importance to Paul, as if he were a lucky rabbit's foot.

"Don't worry," I said, "I'll give him the better-the-agent-you-can-trust-than-the-sharp-chiseler-who-might-do-you-down routine."

"That's good of you, Charlie. You've been a good friend to me."

Everybody's friend, good old Charlie.

15

Paul signed for the Shelley film and got his dollars, and Tony bought himself an E-type Jaguar, and a small house in Chelsea. Stella nailed her part as Harriet. It was a prosperous period, one way and another. Even I could have benefited. I was offered a job by another film company, and five thousand smackers a year, steady stuff, not up and down, like the free-lance work I was doing with Jessie. They wanted me because I had done such a good job on Paul. But I wasn't going to be deflected.

I had evolved my unlikely plan in Durrington, to smash his marriage by making him a star, and I had stuck to it. But until the marriage was busted, and I had scooped up Shirley from the ruins, I didn't feel like leaving the entourage.

It was a surprise to the film people when I refused the job. I told them Konzakis wanted me to do Paul's publicity for the new Shelley film, and so did Paul, and I couldn't let him down, as he was an old friend. You don't often find loyalty like that these days.

They all flew to Italy on location, and during the time they were away I saw little of Shirley, and then only in irreproachable surroundings in London. They say the wife is often the last to hear of her marriage disaster. It was true in her case.

I picked up the name Stella Fenton often enough among gossip writers, and always linked with Paul King. Nothing was printed about a romance. It was early days yet. But I now had solid grounds for believing that for me the moment of triumph was approaching. And now, for the first time, I realized what it was going to mean to Shirley. But I pushed the thought away when it came into my mind.

One evening, I had occasion to see Perry, Konzakis' publicity man. After a while he said, "We're throttling down on the personal angle until after the film. Public's getting a bit tired of film stars and their divorces. They are more routine than news. The oldest of old hat."

Konzakis' spy network had been at work. Perry took a slug of whisky. Odd face he had, quite expressionless, thin and pike-like, and the skin never moved; only his pale eyes had any life, and they held a look of self-mockery.

"It won't be hard to build up a new 'happy marriage of

true minds' image, once the thing's in the bag," he went on.

"If he marries her."

We both knew who "her" was. He didn't say anything.

I asked, "Don't you like Stella?"

"I like what I'm paid to like, see? If I had had any guts I should have stuck to journalism. Selling out is selling out, whichever way you slice it. What's the difference between Stella and a soap powder? Neither of them is kind to the hands."

"What's the film like?"

"I don't think it'll get good write-ups, but it should do the business. Stella's new, and she's not going to be too bad. It should do the business. Romantic slush often does. You're handling the personal bit," he went on. "So for God's sake don't let's have any happy marriage stuff, or pictures of Shirley and the child romping on the lawn."

I could hear from his voice that this was something that had happened to him before.

"Do you think you can stop the magazine ladies interviewing her?"

"I think so. Shirley's not keen on publicity, anyway."

"You know Shirley well?"

His mocking eyes were fixed on me.

"Quite well."

"Yes. I heard you did. So I can leave it to you?"

I told him he could. And I told myself to be careful. I suddenly remembered how, after the Savoy party, when Shirley got plastered, Paul had asked me if I had put her to bed. I'd sensed a trap. I wasn't going to be the fall guy then. I wasn't going to be one now.

So I kept away from her, and never went down to Hampshire, hard though it was.

The reviews were bad when the Konzakis idea of Shelley was sprung on a nearly defenseless audience. Especially in the Sundays. They'd had more space on which to sharpen their typewriters. Example:

"Paul King, as yet another tragic poet, in *The Loves of Shelley* isn't particularly interesting. To depict one of our strangest and most complicated lyric poets, it is not enough to wear Regency trousers, an open necked shirt and a blank stare, dead centre, into the camera. Nor are prickings of conscience delineated by working the jaws very slowly and sadly, as if the subject was thinking his egg wasn't fresh."

That was a cutting I didn't stick in.

Still, there were queues in Leicester Square, and a huge picture of Paul, with a pink face, ultramarine blue eyes, holding a book of verse about two feet square, and chewing the end of a quill pen.

One midday, I walked down to the Salisbury. I hadn't got a lunch date, and decided to have a quick sandwich, because I'd a load of work waiting for me back at the office.

In a corner of the Salisbury, I saw Tony Banks. It struck me as odd. The Salisbury wasn't his kind of beat, he was a Caprice-and-Ritz man. He was sitting on one of the benches near the window, not touching his drink or smoking, looking out of the window. I got my sandwich and glass of beer, and went up to him, and greeted him. He looked up and nodded.

"How's everything?"

I sat down beside him. I felt if I had stuck a pin into him, he wouldn't have noticed.

"Nice queues in Leicester Square, as I came along," I said.

He didn't answer. But eventually he picked up his drink, drank it straight down, and then looked at me.

"I suppose you've heard the news?"

"What news?"

"Paul's sacked me."

I didn't look into his eyes. I just muttered astonishment and regret and asked why. He shrugged his shoulders.

"I think he blamed me for the reviews."

"The film's doing all right."

"That's not the point, is it?"

I suppose he'd been having the great actor routine, poor devil. He didn't even ask my advice, he didn't try and gloss over the facts. It was no use my doing the good old Charlie bit. It was too late for sips of soothing syrup. Paul had finally kicked the stuffing out of him.

"I'm going to see Konzakis about it this afternoon. He's the only man who might have some influence with Paul—don't you think?"

I nodded approvingly. Where the money was, there the influence was.

"Where's Konzakis staying?"

"Down near Brighton."

Yet in my heart, I thought Tony was wasting his time. What difference did it make to Konzakis who handled Paul? Tony was just fringe stuff, like me, expendable. But people cling to any straw. No point in disillusioning them.

We had another drink, and I tried to relax him a bit. He was like a man wound up beyond his capacity and equally capable of action or inaction. One minute he seemed to want to talk about his trouble, and the next he sank into an apathy of indecision. He was a pawn who had imagined he was influencing the game. Some pawns could, but not this one. I walked down the road with him. I wanted to tell him not to go round with his begging bowl, not to put himself in a position of being humiliated.

It was raining on his bald patch. He dropped me at my office and drove off, a man who had lost his lucky rabbit's foot.

It was the last time I saw him.

He never got to see Konzakis at all. His car went into a tree on the Balcombe Road to Brighton. There are still a lot of old forest trees on the Balcombe Road, they have been there a long time.

The coroner said it must have been a damp greasy patch on the road. There was a small amount of alcohol in the body, but nothing which could have accounted for the accident. He was normally a very careful driver. No one could understand it at all. The E-type Jag made a spectacular crash picture. So he must have been going fast. I got Paul's name into all the obituary notices, as I had in Mike Standford's. I know my job all right.

People react differently to misfortune. Tony expressed his emotions in unaccustomed high speed and killed himself. Paul King lashed out, he sacked Tony.

He also sacked his wife.

It came quite suddenly. The rumors involving him and Stella had been growing. The first mention in public was a seemingly innocuous little gossip paragraph in a film magazine:

> Paul King, and Stella Fenton who acted in his last picture, *The Loves of Shelley,* and also played in the Rupert Brooke film, are often seen together at first nights these days. They say that travelling with a friend can either cement or break the friendship. In Paul and Stella's case, it seems to have done the former. She went with him to New York for the première of the Rupert Brooke film and then, of course, on location to Italy for *The Loves of Shelley.* "Paul and I are just good friends," said Miss Fenton last week.

Then the telephone rang one evening, and Paul asked, rather peremptorily, whether I was going to be in for a couple of hours. I had a feeling that sex was raising its ugly head. When people want to see you urgently, it's always sex or money. Their sex or your money. They can always restrain their impatience when it's a question of coughing up the stuff they owe you.

Paul didn't ask me whether he could come round, he just took it for granted that I'd wait in for him. It was pouring with rain.

I'd now found myself a small mews house in Belgravia, and when I opened the front door, he was standing there looking like a lover in a French film. The rain was running off his face in rivulets. He came in, wiped his face, and I saw him looking round the sitting room. Probably totting up the cost of everything, and wondering whether I'd bought the house on a mortgage. But when I spoke to him he didn't answer, as if all his thoughts were focused inwards. I handed him a whisky, and he sat for a long time without saying anything. I wasn't going to prompt him.

"What would you do, Charlie?" he said at last. "It's myself and Shirley."

I looked innocent and concerned, focusing my eyes on his face, but listening to my racing heartbeats.

"You're not going to split up?" I asked in a shocked voice. It was well done. I'd practiced the line often enough.

"No one knows what these things are like until they've been through them!"

It's unfortunate that victims are callous enough to inflict mental suffering on their slayers. It would help socially if they would look more cheerful when they are stabbed in the back. He was feeling a tinge of the pain and humiliation he was to inflict on his wife.

Then it all came out, as was inevitable. The rambling excuses, the self-justification, the unending parcels of badly tied codswallop.

It had all started too early for him.

A man had a right to his own life.

Why should an artist be tied down by domesticity?

Better a clean break; no good making a pattern of unhappiness.

Better for the child, too. Not good for little Jane to be brought up in an atmosphere of strain and dissension. Di-da, di-da.

Tell me the old, old story stuff, I thought.

The bit about the child had to come, of course. I've often noticed this sudden concern for children. Only one thing was missing, and it had to come too, and it did, in the usual ringing tones of one who has sat through too many films.

He ended by saying loudly, "I'm through, I tell you, through!"

I looked thoughtful and wise, and said, "I shouldn't do anything in a hurry, Paul."

He gulped the remains of his whisky and said, "I've done it. I've written her a letter and posted it tonight."

It is always easier to stab by letter. You don't have to watch the victim's face. He got up to go, and said, "I'd like you to go down tomorrow to her, Charlie. Tell her it's no use trying to argue about it. I'm through, see?"

Victims who argue and plead and weep can be distressing. It is not a tactful way of going on.

"Okay, Paul," I said heavily, "I'll go, though I wouldn't do it for anybody but you."

Shortly after, he went out into the rain, and I was left to savor my moment of triumph. This was the end towards which I had worked, the result of all the planning, nurtured by hate and jealousy, yet warmed and sustained by my desire for Shirley. The theory had been sound. The wife had been discarded, the rocket booster cast off in the rise to fame.

For a long while I sat staring at nothing in particular, listening to the excited thudding of my heart.

Next day, the rain had stopped and the sun was shining. I drove down to Shirley, dreading the encounter, yet knowing that it was all for the best.

There was a small breeze, and everywhere there were blossoming trees. The house lay back from the road at the end of a curving drive. It was set down, lower than the road, near Fordingbridge, and like most Tudor houses, was snug against the wind. It was one of those houses which look like a film set, all unexpected corners, part stone, part brick, and yet the whole mellowed into the landscape. As I drove towards the garages, I wondered why Paul hated it. Maybe it looked too enduring.

I walked across the lawn, and found Shirley sitting by the side of the fishpond. She had given up wearing glasses, and taken to contact lenses which threw into focus the extraordinary beauty of her eyes.

"I had a feeling you would come today, Charlie," she said. I sat beside her on the flat stones. "I know why you've come."

I still didn't say anything. She spoke first, in a flat, dead voice.

"You've come to tell me he isn't coming back—ever, and that I might as well accept the fact," she said. "Funny, I thought that when it came to the end I would be sobbing. I'm beyond it. I've cried so much, and so uselessly. They say when surgeons cut off a man's leg, it aches as if it were still there. Yet half of me has gone, and I don't feel a thing."

Her expression was not hard, it was simply remote, like a priest who's found out he doesn't believe in God after all.

"I had a visitor yesterday. Old Vic. He came quite unexpectedly, he was doing a play in Salisbury."

She looked at me again with that remote, colorless look, and said, "He's a nice man, Vic. A good man. It doesn't pay off, does it? He got ditched because his wife wanted a regular meal ticket, and I get ditched because Paul is a success."

I tried to break in, but she wouldn't let me.

"No, it's no use telling me anything else, Charlie. In the end you have to look things straight in the eye. The first time I wore contact lenses, it was a curious feeling. I had never really seen my face while I was making up before. It was just like that the last time Paul came to see me. I felt I had never seen him before either. I suppose I knew it was the last time. Have you ever looked at something quite ordinary with a magnifying glass—say, the shirt you are wearing. It seems clean, but look at it with all the little specks of dirt magnified, and you feel quite differently about it. It's not a pleasant feeling. You feel cheated." She shrugged her shoulders. "I admit it's hard to have believed in someone who never existed. What was the point?"

"Nothing is wasted," I said, lamely. "Things work out."

She looked at me uncertainly. Not believing me. That's the thing the heels of this life do, they take away confidence. It was going to take time to build her up, to make her see and feel that she wasn't a failure. There's a particular bitterness for a woman about being chucked on the scrap heap. It unsexes her. It was going to take time.

It's strange how often actors equate their own lives with

the parts they have played. Shirley now said, "I always thought Queen Katherine, in *Henry VIII,* a bit of a drip. I understand her now. 'Have I not with my full affections still met the king? Lov'd him next heaven? Obey'd him? Been, out of fondness, superstitious to him? And am I thus rewarded? 'Tis not well, lords.' And it isn't, is it, Charlie?"

Even when she spoke with bitterness, her voice had a charm for me, and the perfume of her personality was all round me. How could he throw her away?

For a moment I didn't answer. I could have fallen back on the obvious, and said it was all a rat race, but when I thought of Paul I thought it would be an insult to a highly courageous and intelligent animal.

"I always think," I said, at length, "the great thing in life is to try to behave not *quite* as badly as most people. And that wouldn't be difficult either."

"You're a cynic, Charlie."

"A cynic who is on your side."

"I know that. Is there another woman? Someone he wants to marry?"

I decided to lie and shook my head uncertainly, and then wished I hadn't.

"That's almost more insulting, don't you think? In a way, infidelity isn't terribly important. It's ephemeral. It doesn't alter anything basic, not really."

I knew what she meant. Anyone can fall into bed in an off moment, but what she was facing was a complete betrayal of everything. Like feeling a log was solid, and then finding it hollow, and crawling with worms.

"You are still young, and life can still be beautiful for you," I said tenderly. Pretty corny, but I saw the trembling of her lips and decided to be matter of fact and practical. I asked about financial arrangements.

"I don't want his money," she said bitterly, and got up.

"You've got Jane to think of. I'm not saying money is all important, but it helps."

For the first time, she smiled.

"You sound like Bohun in *You Never Can Tell*—do you remember when you played him at Durrington?"

" *'Insist on a settlement. That shocks your delicacy—most sensible precautions do, but you ask my advice; and I give it to you. Have a settlement!'* " I quoted.

"You should be wearing a false nose."

"Maybe it would improve my face."

"You have a very nice face. Some faces get better as they get older."

Kind, dear Shirley.

We walked back to the house, arm in arm. It looked very comfortable and snug.

On the way, I reverted to the question of alimony, because I had a feeling that Paul would try to get out of it on the cheap. How cheap I did not realize until I asked her point blank. She sighed and said disinterestedly, "He said in his letter he'd give me £1,500 a year, tax free, and the house."

I stopped on the gravel path and stared at her, and burst out angrily, "But that's preposterous! Look at all the money he's earned and will earn!"

"I'm not interested," she said woodenly. "I'm just not interested, see?"

"Well, I *am,*" I said furiously. "You can't let him get away with chicken feed like that—it's a bloody insult!"

She put her hand on my arm, and said gently, "Let's leave it for the moment, Charlie. It'll do me good to have to earn money again. You see that, don't you? It'll take my mind off things. Did you know old Vic has started a little school for coaching people—voice production and all the rest of it? He can give me a few lessons, because I expect I've got a bit rusty. Then I'll try radio again. Maybe, who knows I may get a few small parts in television. Tony Banks might have helped me—"

She began to move on without completing the sentence. She had been fond of Tony. So had we all.

"That's what I'll do," she said, with a sort of pathetic attempt to seem determined, cheerful, and practical. "I'll have some lessons, then I'll go back to show biz—part time, anyway."

I stayed for lunch, and in the afternoon, we took Jane

on a hunt for bluebells. I left Shirley just after tea. She was looking pale and sick, and who wouldn't be.

I didn't discuss the future. I knew that first I had to let the poison of disillusion work out of her system, to let the high emotions seep away, and the dead hand of loneliness seize her.

But now, I noted how, in her agony and distress, a curious change had come over her. Suddenly she had gained in stature and dignity.

She was no longer a soppy date, and I didn't think she ever would be again. She was a personality in her own right, matured and calm.

As I left her I felt that all had indeed been worthwhile.

I telephoned Paul King when I arrived back in London, asking if it was convenient to come and see him the next morning. He ignored my question at first, and asked how Shirley was taking it.

"As well as can be expected."

"Meaning what?"

"Meaning just that—as well as can be expected," I replied, sort of objectively cheerful, like a doctor taking a clinical view of a postoperative case. "When can I come round?"

He hesitated. Like all weak characters, he wasn't keen to hear the grisly details for which he was responsible.

"I'm a bit tied up tomorrow."

I laughed outright, loudly.

"What's so funny?" he asked irritably.

"I should see me," I said ominously, "I should see me, if I were you. If you know what's good for you, I should see me."

Now, at last, I could come into the open. Now I could be myself with him. The chains of restraint were dropping off me, link by link, I could almost hear them clanking to the floor in a heap as I stood by the telephone listening to Paul King wriggling. I had worn them a long time, self-shackled, and sometimes the burden had been almost more than I could bear. Now I could feel the mental circulation gaining strength as I flexed my brain muscles, stretching myself emotionally, luxuriating in my new freedom. The sensation of winning the fight had been dimmed at Shirley's house by the sight of her suffering, but now I was savoring the full flavor and exulting in it.

"Meaning what?" he asked again, repetitiously and tiresomely. I could be repetitous, too.

I said gently, "Just that—I should see me, if you know what's good for you."

I wasn't playing with him like a cat plays with a mouse. I didn't feel like a cat, I felt like a tiger, and I didn't see him as a mouse, I saw him as a goat. Tethered and uneasy. I could hear him bleating uncertainly.

He said, "What about? Shirley?"

"Naturally."

"What about Shirley?"

"I can't tell you on the phone," I said softly.

"Is she being—difficult?"

"It's not Shirley that's going to be difficult."

There was silence for a few seconds. Then he spoke sharply. It was the last time he tried to crack the whip, and now the lash passed harmlessly over my head.

He said, "I am not sure I like your tone, Charlie."

"Well, never mind my tone—when do I see you?"

"I'm driving down to Brighton for lunch tomorrow with Konzakis," he said petulantly.

"When do I see you?" I said stolidly. "If you wish, that is, I don't mind if I don't see you."

The feeling of power is a subtle thing. Others sense it, some fear it, without knowing what they fear. He said uncertainly, "I leave at ten."

"Good old you," I murmured insolently. He knew for certain, then, that he was up against something formidable, and the unknown nature of it made him the more uneasy. I remember thinking that, with his conscience, I was not surprised.

He said, with an assumed sigh, "I could see you for a few minutes before I leave—say at a quarter to ten."

"No good. I have another appointment at ten," I said. "Forget it. Don't bother."

He gave another, deeper sigh. I knew what the sigh meant. It was supposed to be a resigned, preparatory noise, clearing the ground for acceding to an importunate supplication from a peasant, but the trouble was that the peasant was an ex-actor who could recognize another actor when he was acting. I knew I had him on the run.

"All right—come at nine-thirty," he said shortly.

"Nine-fifteen." I imagined him frowning, worried, knowing that something serious was in the air, and compelled to know what it was as soon as possible.

"All right—but it's most inconvenient."

"Too true, it is," I said harshly, and put down the receiver.

That night I slept soundly. Before I put the light out, I said a final goodnight to Good Old Charlie. I wouldn't be seeing him again. In a way, I was sorry to see him go. But he had served his purpose.

I arrived next morning at Arlington House at five past nine, not a quarter past. He had drunk his orange juice, and was nibbling a thin slice of toast Melba as he sipped his coffee.

I didn't take off my overcoat. I went straight into the tarted up living room, and stood by the window, looking down at him.

"It won't do, mate," I said, offensively.

He looked up at me with the old, familiar little-boy-lost look in his gray eyes.

"What won't do, Charlie?"

As an act to hide his hidden uneasiness, his fear of the unknown, it was reasonably good. I could have done better, given a chance, in my acting days. I would have played it more aggressively. But these parts depend upon how the actor interprets them. Meanwhile, in the present instance, I had the advantage—because I had no longer a role to play. I was simply Charles Maither, myself, free and raring to go.

"Your suggested alimony terms—bloody mean and unacceptable," I replied, crisp and businesslike.

"Mean? Fifteen hundred a year, tax free, and the house?"

he said, wide eyed. Surprised innocence. Slightly hurt look. I knew the routine. Dead easy to a pro.

"Unacceptable."

"I wouldn't have thought Shirley was like that," he said carefully, and took a sip of coffee.

"She isn't—I am."

He said, "Ah," and put down his coffee cup and pushed back the Regency chair, and walked over to the fireplace, across the thick golden carpet, and turned and looked at me.

"Charlie, you mustn't meddle between man and wife. She is still my wife—but as from this minute you are no longer my public relations man, you will realize that?"

"Too true I'm not," I said happily. He made a vague gesture towards the door.

"Then there's no more to be said."

"Yes, there is—plenty."

He went through the old, dreary, go-away-little-man-I'm-busy routine, sighing wearily, and all that malarky.

"Charlie, I'm in rather a hurry."

I sat down in the chair he had vacated and began munching a slice of his toast Melba. I said, "I'm negotiating for Shirley. You can keep the house and contents. I value it at £15,000, contents £5,000. And she'll forgo all regular alimony. She'll settle for £60,000—plus the £20,000 for the house and contents. Say £80,000. Paid now, by crossed check, made out to her, and you can give me a covering note, too. I'll take it round to her bank when I leave you. Clean break, see? You can go to Brighton this morning with a light heart. All fixed up in a friendly way. No sordid haggling. Right?"

I was looking out of the window as I spoke. Casual stuff. Watching a woman walk her white poodle round the block, listening to the noise of the traffic below, with one ear, listening for the response with the other. After a moment, I looked round at him, exulting, because I knew I was hitting him on his weak spot. He was always mean about money. He began to move towards the house phone. Bluffing, of course, and I knew he was bluffing and he knew I knew it, but he had to go through the routine. Once an actor always an actor.

"You'd better go, Charlie, or I'll have you thrown out. You're not welcome here. You're trespassing."

"Go on," I taunted him, "lift the receiver, what's stopping you? Have me thrown out, boyo. If you hurry up, it'll make the lunchtime editions. You want to get a move on, you do."

Thus, for a few moments, we did our little mocking war dance, each against each, and each at heart recognizing it for what it was, a fluffing out of feathers, a preliminary skirmish, a belligerent feinting.

He'd abandoned the little-boy-lost look. He had a little-boy-in-a-temper look, and it wasn't faked this time. His lips were compressed. He wasn't white with rage, as the old cliché goes, but he was pretty yellow, and his eyelids had dropped over his eyes, as in the old days when he was thinking out propositions or brooding about the small print in a contract.

He turned away from the phone impatiently and swung round and I saw a slight flicker in his eyes, the beginning of a malicious smile at the corners of his mouth. They were gone almost before I could register them, but they put me on the alert. I felt he was going to have a real swipe at me in a minute, and so he did, but though I was expecting something, the nature of it took me unawares.

For the moment, he contented himself with saying, "I don't propose to negotiate with you, Charlie. I shall tell Shirley so. And so that we know where we stand I shall tell her now."

He had reached the telephone and lifted the receiver before I could speak. I heard him ask for her number. I said abruptly, desperately, because I couldn't think of anything else, "Pity you can't ring Beryl Wilson, isn't it?"

He slammed the receiver down and stared at me.

"Beryl who?"

"Wilson, Beryl Wilson of Accringham. Your old girl friend who—died. You forgotten her? I'm surprised you've forgotten her," I said gently. "Funny, isn't it? One moment a girl is there. Then she's gone. Then she's forgotten. Well, that's show biz," I murmured acidly. "Except she wasn't in show biz. Cancel the call to Shirley."

We stared at each other for some seconds. I never felt more confident. Doubtless he read it in my face. I watched him lift the receiver and cancel the call.

I said, "That's better, isn't it? Now we can chat like old friends."

He walked over to me, and I got to my feet. He said, "As you know so much, you'll know the coroner exonerated me from all blame. She was highly neurotic. Have you anything to add?"

I knew where I was going, I knew we were getting to the crunch, but I had to be careful. I didn't put it past him to have a tape recorder hidden somewhere in the room.

Down in the street, the woman with the white poodle was still walking it around, hopefully, pausing every time it wanted to sniff at something.

"I've got nothing to add," I said innocently. "Why should I have? I've got nothing to add at all, except that you seem to be accident prone, that's all I've got to add."

He was standing by a small Sheraton table on which stood an alabaster cigarette box with gold edges and an Indian dagger with an ornate handle. But I didn't think there'd be any nonsense with the dagger, I didn't think that at all, not seriously, though the idea flashed through my mind. His hand was so near it, almost touching it.

He was very close to me, his face unpleasantly yellow, his eyes, gray and unblinking, staring into mine. He said harshly, "What do you mean by that—accident prone?"

"See that white poodle in the street—lifting a leg now and again. Its owner stops whenever the poodle stops. It probably thinks it's a free agent. It hardly feels the lead and collar. Accident prone people are like that dog. They think they're free. But things happen to them. They kind of attract disaster."

This was where I had to be careful, in case of a hidden tape recorder. Blackmail is a serious crime even when committed on somebody else's behalf.

I heard him say, "I don't attract disaster, I attract success—you ought to know, considering the money you've made out of me."

I looked him straight in the face and said, "Beryl Wilson didn't commit suicide. She was murdered. Strangled. The police think so—now. I know a man who knows a man in the Accringham police, see?"

I watched him lick his lips, saw his Adam's apple rise and fall twice in his throat as he swallowed.

"Murdered—what do you mean murdered?"

"It's a simple enough word."

I deliberately turned my back on him and the Sheraton table and the cigarette box and the Indian dagger, and walked a step or two away, and said, "I won't distress you with the theory. She was alone in the house, you remember? But of course you remember! You'll remember that all right, if there's one thing you'll remember it's that she was alone in the house. Somebody went there and killed her. No window was forced, nor was the door. She let him in, see? Probably somebody she knew quite well. I thought I'd let you know so that you'll feel better about it, in a way. She didn't commit suicide because you wrote breaking things off, see? She was killed, see? Strangled while she was alone in the house, alone except for her murderer, of course—whoever he was."

I was walking softly up and down the room now. He was at the window, probably staring down at the white poodle. My heart was beating pretty fast, partly because I'd got the bastard where I wanted him, alone, man to man, separated from Shirley, the years of deception finished, and partly because I was watching my step, picking my words and phrases for this, the softening up process, before I put the squeeze on for the £ 80,000.

"What are you getting at?" he said, almost in a whisper.

"I'm getting at eighty thousand pounds for Shirley, that's what I'm getting at," I said, coldly.

"Whatever you were getting at, you can get out," he said abruptly. "Get out, now. I mean it."

He walked towards the door. I said, "I'll take the check

with me. Made out to her, with a covering note to your bank. I'll pay it in when I leave here. And don't try and stop it later."

He stood with his hand on the door knob, looking round at me.

"Come on," he said. "Out."

He almost managed to exude an implication of inner strength, which shows that bad actors can have their moments, especially when they feel something deeply, like handing out large sums of money. I moved towards the door.

"With check?"

"Without check."

I nodded amicably, but once again I caught that hint of a malicious gleam in his eyes, though now I didn't know if it was due to something he was cooking up or because he thought he had triumphed.

"Okay, if that's the way you want it," I said. "And to show we can still be friends, I'll make you a farewell present — a publicity article, for old time's sake, free, no charge. How's that for friendship? Good old Charlie's parting present."

He let his hand fall from the door knob. He could smell danger now, all right. He'd have been a moron if he couldn't. It was hot and strong in the air.

"One for a British national newspaper, and another, re-written, for America, with simultaneous release dates," I said thoughtfully.

"On what lines?" he asked suspiciously.

"The usual stuff — only a bit more so. Actor's triumph over adversity. That line, see? Sympathetic stuff. Unfortunate childhood conditions. Parents' unhappy marriage. Drunken father runs away, abandoning wife and child. All that."

He was standing by the door, staring at me, fearing what was coming next, hoping that it wouldn't.

"Good stuff," I said cheerfully. "Make the headlines. Star's father died in mental asylum. How his frail mother worked her fingers to the bone to support them both. Threadbare clothes, rent troubles. No toys, No holidays. Old mother's present ill health due to those days. But old mother still working. Does not want to be a burden. Then I'll get on to you personally," I said, cheerfully, "Paul King's own early struggles. His first love, Beryl Wilson, and her tragic end. His marriage. A child. His marriage breaks up. His triumphs and, to balance the picture, just a brief passing reference to Hamlet at Stratford. As told by his friend, Charles Maither. I'll have them weeping in the aisles at all your sufferings!" I ended enthusiastically.

He moved from the door, across the room to the window and stood looking out, near the Sheraton table with the alabaster cigarette box and the Indian dagger, and said, "If you publish that, I'll sue you."

"Sue me?" I said, surprised. "What for? Why, the why I'll write it, you'll have every middle-aged woman in Britain and America wanting to mother you!"

I followed him across to the window and said softly in his ear, "Tell you what I'll do—I'll cut out the reference to the Hamlet disaster. How's that?"

He swung round to face me. He was taller than me, well built and probably fit, for he had dieted for the Shelley film, hardly drank and had given up smoking. As he faced me, white faced, taut, I could detect no soft lines anywhere in his face. He is a killer, I thought. By God, he is a killer all right. I felt no fear but for a moment I felt sick. I was not afraid, because I did not think he would try to kill me. But I felt sick because I had a fearful vision of how I would feel if I had been a young woman and looked up at him and seen his face, and pleaded and seen no compassion anywhere in the big, staring blue eyes.

He said, "That's not the image I want! And you bloody well know it."

"It's the image you'll get," I said unemotionally, and stepped a little away from him. "The pictures will be good, too. Your birthplace, humble—perhaps even sordid. Your mother, Edith, smoking, of course. The mental asylum where your father died. Beryl Wilson—I'll hunt up her parents, I think, and get a few paragraphs on 'The Tragic Romance.' How it started, what went wrong, all that crap. Finally,

171

a few understanding remarks by Shirley. Simple little wife stuff. How she only wants you to be happy, and all that. Good, eh?"

"There's talk of a new Byron film," he said violently. "How the hell do you expect me to get the part if you publish all that? Especially after the Shelley flop."

"Do I really mind? Do I feel it here?" I asked, tapping my heart. "Tell, do I really care, Buster?"

I could hear his mind going tick-tock, calculating his possible future earnings from Byron, his money in the bank or in securities, what a Court might award Shirley if she went to Court for proper alimoney.

"Blackmail?" he said.

"The public has a right to know about the idols upon whom it lavishes so much money," I replied sanctimoniously, ever conscious of a possible tape recorder.

"How can I be sure she won't accept a lump sum and later demand alimony as well?"

"You can't. But she won't. You know that."

But he shook his head, and said, "No lump sum. You can tell her that, with my compliments."

I said it wouldn't do, and that I would now go back to my office and write the articles, since that was the way he wanted it.

It was, of course, blackmail, and pretty crude at that.

He said nothing for a few moments, and I thought I was going to win. Then he said, well, he would raise the alimony offer to £2,000 a year, but keep the house, and that was final, and it was generous. His hesitation seemed to confirm the inner core of weakness I always suspected. I thought I only had to push a little harder, and I turned as if to go to the door.

But weak men are unpredictable. They cave in most of the time, and then suddenly, usually in the wrong place, they dig their toes in. He flushed again, and said, all right, then publish and be damned, the corny quote from the Wellington and Harriet Wilson row. I suggested he think again, and we got rather heated and there was a certain amount of argy-bargy.

172

Finally, I said, "I don't trust you. The only thing I trust is your money. Shirley built you up, coached you, supported you morally, and sometimes with the cash she earned. She's entitled to a fair cut of the fortune you've raked up. But if she marries again you'll apply to the Court for a cancellation of alimony, that's what you'll do, and if you don't get it, you'll get a big reduction. That's what might happen, and that's what I don't want to see happen. I want her to have a fair share of your earnings."

Any moderate actor can produce a scornful little sneer at the drop of a hat. He produced one now. But if the sneer was plastic, the malice in his eyes wasn't. Whatever he had cooked up, he judged the time was now ripe to serve it.

"I'm sure you do, Charlie."

"Meaning what?"

I was so innocent of mercenary motives that the heavy sarcasm in his voice puzzled me.

"I'm not a fool, Charlie," he said softly.

"That's a matter we can debate some other time."

"I know perfectly well that after the divorce you'll try to marry Shirley. Poor old Charlie."

"Go on," I said.

"Do I need to?"

I nodded, because I could not speak. All the pent-up fury and jealousy of the years was about to be set alight by what I saw was coming.

It had started to rain and there were occasional little gusts of wind which hurled the rain against the windows. Above the hiss and spatter of the rain, and the drone of cars below, I heard his voice, and it seemed to be coming from some distance, because there was a third noise, and that was the noise of blood in my ears produced by my thudding heart beats. I remember his exact words:

"She wouldn't taste so sweet without the alimony, would she, Charlie? A capital sum, like a thing of beauty, can be a joy forever, can't it? With her money—or should I say mine?—and your imagination, you should be all right, sitting pretty, you'd be, Charlie, except that you won't get it."

Part Three
On Track, Off Track

16

Y*ou come back and wander around Durrington years after it is all over, seeking the truth and whether, and if so how, you were to blame.*

You decide, over and over again, that you feel no guilt about the actual killing of Paul King.

It was not on the agenda.

An item which is not on the agenda should not have to be considered. Yet, all the while you are considering it.

Your mind goes back to the moments of crisis. You are glad now, as you were then, that there is no longer a death penalty in England, because you had a personal interest.

As you wander around, you recall that somewhere, some time, somebody said that immediately prior to his execution, a man would eagerly settle for permanent life-long solitary confinement on the top of a tower, cut off forever from human contact.

You see again the Theatre Royal, the other landmarks, you remember the Inspector and the Sergeant, and how things went. And you agree.

You'd settle for the top of the tower.

A uniformed police constable abruptly opened the door, half came into the room, saw it was occupied and withdrew hastily, with a muttered apology. Neither the Chief Inspector nor the Sergeant took any notice. They were both staring at me, the Inspector watchful but unemotional.

The Sergeant was doing his hostile, alert, ginger Tom cat act. You could almost see his ears pricked forward, his eyes smoldering. Even his head was lowered for a spring.

"Go on," I said aggressively, because I was afraid. "Ask me what you like, I don't care, I've got nothing to hide."

The Sergeant gave a laugh. The Inspector leaned back in his chair and sighed, like one who is no longer surprised by human actions and human lies.

"You don't want to get pettish," the Sergeant said.

The Inspector took two pieces of paper out of the folder in front of him. I tensed myself, knowing that no good for me could come out of that folder.

"I propose to read you an extract from a signed statement made by Mrs. Paul King, better known to you as Shirley King. In her statement, she says: 'I was visited by Mr. Charles Maither on the day before my husband died. The conversation was mainly concerned with the break-up of my marriage. Mr. Maither expressed himself as greatly concerned about the financial arrangements which my husband had proposed for me. He was highly indignant. I told him it was a matter of indifference to me, but he remained highly indignant. I admit that for some time, Mr. Maither has, I think, been in love with me.'"

The Inspector tossed the statement back into the folder, and inched forward his chair. For several moments he said nothing.

The Sergeant picked up his cheap wooden pencil. The end of my cigarette was pointed and red, because I was tapping away the ash, unnecessarily, after each puff. The Inspector said, "You are aware that Mr. King left a will, made two or three years ago?"

"Did he?"

The Inspector pushed his chair back suddenly, and walked to the window, and stood looking out of it. The Sergeant watched intently. Without turning round, the Inspector said, "Did he? You say, did he? You ought to know, sir, you witnessed it."

I remembered then. It was one night after his West End play had started to pick up. It was a simple will, of the kind you can buy cheaply in a stationer's shop.

"That's right—I remember now," I said.

"You remember now? That's something."

"That's something he remembers," muttered the Sergeant.

"You knew the contents?"

"Of course not—except that there was nothing in it for me," I said quickly, "otherwise I couldn't legally have witnessed it."

The Inspector said, still with his back to me, "As all wills are eventually available to the public, I will inform you now that he left one quarter of his property to his mother for her lifetime, and the remainder to his wife. I assume you knew it would be something like that? I assume Mrs. King knew it, and recently realized she would be a very wealthy woman in the case of his death—provided she was still married to him at the time?"

I watched him turn from the window and walk slowly back to his chair, and said nothing, because fear is a strange thing. It either makes you talk too volubly, or it shuts you up, so that you cannot say a word. Or, indeed, do anything, except stare.

Now, suddenly, he extracted from his folder a piece of thick white writing paper. He held it across the table, so that I could see the writing.

"Recognize that?"

I nodded. It was a letter Shirley had written to me before Paul's death. I didn't know how the Inspector had found it. A desperate little letter. To me, who knew her, it was the last sad threshings around of a loyal worker bee caught in honey. I don't know why I kept it. Just because it was from Shirley, I suppose. He threw it across the table to me. I picked it up, though I knew the gist of it. It read:

Darling Charlie,

I've done my best but it doesn't work. He doesn't

react at all. I might just as well have saved my efforts. It's up to you now, Charlie—if you can do it.

All my love, Shirley.

I put it down carefully on the table between us, and heard the Inspector say, "Quite an affectionate letter, one way and another."

"Oh, for God's sake," I said impatiently. "'Darling' means nothing in the theatre world!"

"How was her husband supposed to react, and didn't?" the Sergeant asked, and stared at me in his usual predatory way. If his hands hadn't been occupied with pencil and notebook, they would have been kneading the table, claws sinking into the surface. And now a transformation came over the Inspector, too. He became rougher, and, in a way, more crude, as if he'd done with playing around and was launched on a main assault.

He repeated part of the Sergeant's question. "How was this unfortunate gentleman, Mr. Paul King, supposed to react? Drop dead?"

"Drop dead?" repeated the Sergeant, and he wasn't speaking lightly. "What didn't he react to? How was he supposed to react?"

"Why was she appealing for help—go on, tell us that," said the Inspector. They'd dropped all the "sir" stuff now. I banged the table to stop them doing the one-two act.

The cat Sergeant said, "Stop banging the table."

"Stop going on at me!" I shouted. The Sergeant put on a surprised aggrieved look.

"Who's going on at you? I'm not going on at you, the Inspector's not going on at you, nobody's going on at you."

"It's simple enough," I began, but he wouldn't let me finish.

"It'll be the only thing that *is* simple. Go on, then."

"Mrs. King had been trying to console Paul King for the bad Shelley notices, and she hadn't had any success. She was asking me to do what I could. She didn't want him to go on being upset. She thought if she could make him happier, perhaps he—"

My voice trailed away. It was clear enough to me, what I wanted to say, but I couldn't find the words.

"Letters like that can cause a lot of trouble," the Inspector said quietly, and I knew he was watching the perspiration which was once more gathering on my forehead.

"In certain circumstances, they do," the Sergeant added. "Such as when a wife and her lover both know there's a lot of money coming to the wife, if the husband dies."

"Provided he dies before there is a divorce," the Inspector said casually, not looking at me, looking at the nail on his right thumb. "It's a pity letters like that get written."

"Ought to be a law against it," the Sergeant said, and smirked, glancing at the Inspector.

I looked at the outside world, over the Inspector's shoulder. The sky was gray and ominous. It was not getting dark yet, but the heart of the day was dying. I had a sudden flash of memory, back over the years, right back to my boyhood, to the tragic Edith Thompson, who had been hanged, for complicity in the murder of her husband by her youthful lover. It was her silly, over-dramatic letter about her imaginary failure to poison him with ground glass which led her to the gallows. Money wasn't involved, just passion, but the end would have been the same, the end had been the noose.

A pigeon was strutting to and fro on the window sill. I thought, in the City of London, they try everything to keep pigeons and starlings off windows sills. The latest idea was jelly. The insecurity of landing on jelly was supposed to discourage the birds. But the discouraged birds let fall droppings on the jelly, eventually making it firm, and you were back to square one. But I wasn't a pigeon. My landings grew ever more insecure. I envied the pigeons and starlings.

The perspiration on my brow grew cold. I wiped it away, and almost at once had a short bout of shivering. They looked at me, neither pityingly nor gloatingly, just woodenly.

The Inspector said, "You didn't know the contents of Mr. King's will—either when you witnessed it, or later?"

"Certainly I didn't."

"And you suggest that the woman, Shirley King, didn't know it—either at the time you witnessed it, or later?"

That was a police touch all right, "the woman, Shirley King." I could imagine them discussing the case, always referring to Shirley as "the woman, Shirley King,"saying "the woman, Shirley King" knew what was in the will, "the woman, Shirley King" egged him on to it, "the woman, Shirley King" knew she'd lose most of the money if there was a divorce before he died.

I said, suddenly angry again, angry at the discourtesy of the phrase, angry at the trap set for me, "I never suggested that 'the woman, Shirley King,' as you call her, didn't know what was in the will."

"But you insist that you parted from the husband, Paul King, on friendly terms?"

"Yes," I said bleakly.

"You'll go into the witness box and give evidence to that effect?"

"Yes," I said again, because I had to.

The Inspector glanced at the Sergeant, who nodded slightly. Something had gone wrong somewhere. Something I had said had confirmed something they suspected. I felt the fever in me rising to my cheeks again, so that my face once more glowed guiltily.

The Inspector looked at the Sergeant and said, "He's not being frank and open, Sergeant."

"Boxing and coxing, sir," agreed the Sergeant.

"Shifty," the Inspector said, ignoring me.

"You give 'em a chance, Sergeant, you do your best for 'em, show 'em how to make the best of things, indicate the best way out for 'em, but they go on being shifty."

"Boxing and coxing," said the Sergeant again.

You don't think clearly when you've got a fever. Driven into a corner, you lash out, because you don't much care, you feel tired, you want to get to bed, any bed.

"That letter's my property," I suddenly said. "How did you get hold of it? Legally, that letter is mine."

The Inspector pushed Shirley's letter across the table.

"Keep it," he said. "I have a photographed copy and an affidavit certifying it to be a true copy. Keep the original — if it'll do you any good."

I shook my head, letting Shirley's letter lie on the table.

"How did you get it?" I asked wearily, but almost at once I knew the answer. Consciously try to remember something, and you'll often fail. Let the mind roam, unfettered, as when tired, and the answer comes. I was tired. The answer came. And the answer shocked me.

I realized, with a curious feeling of indignation, that I had been under suspicion, indeed under direct though discreet surveillance, almost from the day of Paul King's death.

"It is the duty of dry cleaners, as indeed all citizens, to assist the police," the Inspector said primly. "In the course of routine inquiries, it was ascertained that you had left a suit to be cleaned at your normal dry cleaners, a few days after Mr. King's death, and that this letter had been found in an inside breast pocket."

The precise, formal phraseology sounded as though it had been learnt by heart from a book of instructions on how to talk to suspects. In contrast with the earlier interrogation, the stilted sentences should have been a warning to me, but they weren't, and I just nodded.

"It is perhaps my duty to inform you that a routine examination of your suit revealed certain traces of blood of the group know as Group AB. I should inform you that this is a very rare blood group, and that Mr. Paul King's blood belonged to this group. Have you anything which you wish to say about this fact?"

Now, at last, the formality of the tone of voice, as much as the sterility of his words came through to me. I knew it was the end of the road. There comes a time, sooner or later — later, if you are fit, sooner, if you are unwell — when you know that you have to bail out. Jettison the aircraft, jump into the dark unknown, hope for the best, make what you can of what comes.

I took a deep breath, stubbed out my cigarette and said, "Okay — I hit him."

I saw them exchange glances, knowing the meaning of the glances, knowing that each was saying to the other, "Now he's cracking, now he's on the run, now we must press him, and not let up."

"You hit him?" the Inspector said.

I nodded, staring at him defiantly.

"You parted on friendly terms, but you hit him?"

"We didn't part on friendly terms—I hit him," I muttered. "But I didn't shoot him."

"Just now you said you would go into the witness box and swear on oath that you parted on friendly terms."

"I am now telling the truth," I said stolidly.

"Same as you were before—still willing to go into the witness box?"

"And swear the opposite, this time?" jeered the Sergeant. "Is that it? How many times did you hit him?"

"I tried to hit him three times, but only two blows connected."

"Where?"

I shook my head and said, irritably, "Does it matter, does it really matter?"

"Everything matters, everything matters now," snapped the Sergeant. "So where?"

"Once with my left fist—below the pelvis. It winded him. His head came forward and I hit him with my right hand on the left side of the face, where the nose joins the mouth. That's all."

"You said three times."

"I tried to hit him a third time, with my left hand, but he was falling back."

"You wanted to hit him a third time?"

I felt myself getting angry. I'd surrendered. I didn't see the point of the questions, and said sarcastically, "Look, if I tried to hit him, you can take it that I *wanted* to—can't you?"

The Inspector sat upright in his chair and said sharply, "What happened—after you'd hit him?"

I shrugged. I wasn't interested. I felt listless, willing to let events take their course. During the rest of the time I was with them I didn't perspire any more, or shiver, or feel the fever flush in my cheeks. I guessed that a murder charge would come, and being resigned to it, I felt no more emotion. Nothing now seemed to matter. Not even Shirley. I was spent, emotionally and physically.

"He fell, crashed on to the side table, lay on the floor a few seconds," I said. "I helped him up because I thought he might have knocked his head. But he hadn't. He was all right, except that he was bleeding from the nose. I left him then."

"And you left without anything further happening?"

I nodded, and lit another cigarette. The flame no longer trembled.

The Sergeant said, "Just shook his hand, I suppose, and wished him the best of British good luck?"

I looked at him and said nothing. He probably saw the dislike in my eyes. He pressed the point. "You didn't say anything, you just helped him to his feet, and went out? Right?"

"If you want to know, I said, 'Serves you bloody well right,' and then went out."

I felt the tension in the room slacken. The Inspector said, almost gently, "You'd better make another signed statement now. If you wish, that is. Shall I suggest the points you cover? No persuasion, just a few helpful suggestions, see?"

"To save time," said the Sergeant. "Avoid subsequent questions—all that."

I nodded. I heard the Inspector say from a distance, "You could start off by saying, 'I, Charles Maither, now wish to amend my previous statement.' You can write it out by hand, or the Sergeant here will take it down and you can sign it. Which do you want?"

"I'll write it by hand," I muttered.

He pulled open a drawer and produced some sheets of foolscap paper and said, "The points you want to cover are these. You weren't really his friend, but—you may like to add — as he was dead, you didn't want to say anything against him — right? You admit that at the last talk you had with him, you put on a spot of pressure — right?"

"No need to mention blackmail," the Sergeant said abruptly. "It's a nasty word. Juries don't like it."

"Juries?" I said quickly. But I suppose I shouldn't have been surprised.

"Never mind that," the Inspector said. "Don't take any notice of the Sergeant. He's impetuous."

He thought for a moment, then said, "You may wish to add that Mr. Paul King insulted you, by wrongly implying that your only interest in prompt cash for his wife was because you planned to marry her after the divorce — right?"

"So you hit him," added the Sergeant. "You could say you didn't mention it in your first statement because you were afraid, in view of what later happened to Mr. King. You could say that."

"If you wish to," the Inspector said, hesitated, and added, "It gets round a lying first statement." I looked at them, from one to the other, astonished and confused. Neither of them any longer had the hunting look. Curiously, having won, having as good as solved their case, being certain now that I had not only hit Paul King but shot him afterwards, being sure that a jury would come to the same conclusion, even though no weapon had been found in my possession, they were almost compassionate, willing to help me make the best of a hopeless defense. The official job being done, a spark of humanity could be allowed to glow, briefly, before they gave evidence in court.

The telephone rang. The Sergeant answered and handed the instrument over to the Inspector. I heard him say, "Yes, sir," once or twice, and, "We're talking to him now, sir," and then "Very good, sir." He replaced the receiver and looked at the Sergeant, saying, "That was the Assistant Commissioner inquiring after Mr. Maither's health."

"Tenderly, sir?"

"That's right."

Suddenly, abruptly, I said, "I think you're going to charge

me with the murder of Paul King. If so, get on with it. I'm fed up."

The Inspector got to his feet and went to the door and called to somebody and had a few whispered words with whoever it was. The man, a uniformed police constable came into the room. The Inspector said to me, "The Sergeant and I will leave you to write your amended statement. You are naturally free to add what you wish. The police constable will stay with you."

"In case you need anything," said the Sergeant sarcastically, and smiled.

They went out of the room. I wrote a brief statement, largely along the lines suggested. Then I sat back and waited. The police constable was young. He seemed embarrassed and tried to talk about the weather, but the chat petered out. I sat listening for the others to return, dreading their return, yet wanting to get it all over and done with.

When they came back, I could read nothing in their faces. But they didn't sit down. I got to my feet, ready to go with them. The Inspector took my new statement. Then he said, coldly, "I do not require to question you further today, but I would be grateful if you would inform me if you wish to leave London during the next seven days."

He and the Sergeant stood aside to let me leave the room.

I don't know what I said as I left the room. I think it was something fatuous, like, "Good evening, then—I'll be around if you want me." I do know that they didn't say anything in reply. They just nodded curtly. A police constable went with me to the front doors. In Victoria Street, I thought of calling a taxi, but didn't. It was getting dark and it was drizzling with rain, and I had a chill. Yet the unexpected fresh air, the smell of freedom, was good to the nostrils. I decided to make my way across St James's Park, and get a taxi in Pall Mall. But reaction set in almost as soon as I had crossed Bird Cage Walk, and I sat down on a bench, feeling suddenly weak.

I lit another cigarette and looked around. Some distance

away, I saw two figures settle themselves on another bench. For me there was some reason to sit on a bench in the park, in the dusk, in the rain. Who else would choose to do so?

I got up after a few minutes, retraced my steps to Victoria Street, and took a taxi back to my flat. I let myself in, lit the electric fire, and mixed myself a whisky and soda. After a while, I got up from my chair and drew the curtains. Before doing so, I glanced up the mews. About twenty yards away, in the entrance to a garage, I noted the glow of a cigarette end.

I suppose they thought, having seen me home for the night, it was safe to light up and relax. The Inspector had not lost interest. I sighed, and went out into the hall and took the evening paper from the letter-box, expecting to find the front page filled with news of wars and rumors of wars, and the United Nations, and strikes and economic crises. But I was wrong. The front page headlines shouted a familiar name at me, and though the news connected with the name shocked me, I felt no emotion other than shock. The headlines said:

KONZAKIS SHOT DEAD
Film Director Found Murdered
in Brighton Flat

The actual facts were brief.

It seemed that he had been found dead by a secretary, returning for work after lunch. People in a neighboring flat had heard nothing. The police were treating it as a case of murder. That was all. The rest of the story consisted of an account of his career, together, inevitably, with a reference to the killing of Paul King, some months previously, and the part which Konzakis had played in turning Paul into an star.

For a long time, I sat in front of the fire, drinking whisky, feeling the chill and the tension beginning to ebb away. Thinking of Durrington, and my great scheme, and all that had happened since. On the table by my side was a letter, in Shirley's handwriting, which I had found on my return. I delayed opening it for a while, savoring in advance the pleasure of reading a letter from her. Then after mixing another whisky, I opened it. The letter, written in her untidy handwriting, was not very long. It said:

Darling Charlie,
I have known, subconsciously for months and months, even before Paul said he'd leave me, that I needed somebody to look after me, so although Paul has not been dead all that long, I am not deciding this on the rebound, as it were.
The fact is, that in due course, Vic Jones and I are going to get married. Darling Charlie, I think I know how you feel about me, but I am rather a silly creature, really, and you are clever and cynical and worldly, and I know I would get on your nerves in the end. You need a cleverer wife than me. Darling Charlie, forgive me if I am hurting you. I know you will get over it and one day see that I am right. Bless you.
Your very fond Shirley.

At first, of course, I couldn't believe what I read. By the time I'd read it three times I knew it was true.
I don't know how long I sat without moving. Maybe an hour, maybe more. I did not feel like weeping, or laughing bitterly, or indeed anything. I felt numbed, except for the pain in my stomach. Sometimes, even now, I still feel a little of the pain. But very little.
Such was the end of all the plotting, the treachery, the heartache and the violence.
Almost as ironic as her decision, was Vic's telephone call, later that evening. I recall his voice, filled with innocent happiness, as he announced the news—and as he said he wanted me to be his Best Man.
How could I refuse dear old Vic Jones?
I stared into the fire, thinking that for the second time I was to be present when Shirley was married.
But meanwhile something else had occurred.

There was a ring at the front door. I went to open it. Joe Gross stood outside in the rain. He looked bedraggled and pale, and came in without being invited and stood in the hall. I asked him to take his coat off and come into the sitting room. But he refused.

Instead, he took an Army type revolver out of his coat pocket. I saw it was fitted with a silencer.

Maybe I looked scared. I felt it. But he said I wasn't to worry. For some months he had been, he thought, rather ill. He had been watching himself doing things which actually he hadn't been doing.

For instance, he had been watching himself grow very bitter about Paul King and Konzakis, because they had plotted to ruin him, and had in fact, succeeded. Tony Banks had been in the plot, too, but Tony had had his punishment meted out in other ways. But not the other two.

That was what Joe Gross said, standing in the hall, holding the revolver with the silencer.

He insisted that he himself had not killed Paul King and Konzakis, he had just watched his other self kill them, because they were bad, evil men. Had I got that clear?

I nodded. I had indeed got it clear. Far clearer than he imagined. I, too, had watched myself doing a strange thing, one evening on top of a big building in New York, by a safety wall with a gap in it, and boards across the gap, and Paul standing there giddy because of the height.

He said he had watched himself kill them, but he himself had not killed them. He had watched himself, as an American citizen and entitled to bear arms, get a silencer he had used in a film, once, and make very clever plans to kill Paul King and Konzakis.

Still, he had been a witness to the crime, and he felt some blame in not coming forward to the police. Now he wished to go to the police.

"Then go to them, Joe, boy, go to them," I said gently.

His dark, big eyes, which had been a little clouded, suddenly shone clear and intelligent. He stood quite still, a small sallow figure, the gun drooping from his hand.

"Come with me, Charlie," he pleaded. "I'm afraid to go to the police alone. I might not even get there."

I got my coat. We went out. Along the mews, two men were still standing in a doorway.

"We don't need to go to a police station, Joe, boy," I said quietly. "These gentlemen will help you."

To the detectives, I said, "This is Mr. Joe Gross. Mr. Gross wishes to give you a revolver, and go with you and help the police about the cases of Mr. Paul King and Mr. Konzakis. Okay?"

I saw them hesitate, but Joe took his gun out of his pocket again and gave it to one of them. The other said, awkwardly, "All right, Mr. Gross, we'll walk along with you to the station, shall we?"

They closed in quickly on each side of him, hands lightly on his elbows.

As they turned to go, Joe smiled at me and said, "Thanks, Charlie."

Good old Charlie, everybody's friend.

I watched him walk down the mews between the two police officers. A small figure, and, as usual, getting smaller all the time.

17

Nothing more in Durrington. It was a long time ago. Nothing at all in Durrington, now. All over.

After wandering around the old haunts, filled with pain and bitterness, I found myself outside the theatre again. It was still locked for lunch, silent and drab in the pale sunshine. No more ghosts. Shirley and Paul, and Vic, and Sarah, and Geoffrey Glover, and all the others, gone now, and I know from experience that you can't recall them, effec-

tively, to the same place on the same day. The second performance is always weak, a watered-down repetition which disappoints.

I hurried away.

Only the journey back to London, now, calling briefly at the George Hotel, Elton, ten miles distant. Clouds gathering in the south. The final confrontation with my conscience was over.

I did not actually kill Paul King. Yet I killed him all the same. I set in train the sequence of events which ended in his death, and in the death of Konzakis, and, come to that, in the death of Tony Banks, and the ruin of Joe Gross.

Such things were not on the agenda, yet they happened. But you go back, defiantly, you face the facts, and because they were not on the agenda, you leave Durrington, and you feel you were a heel, but you don't feel a murderous heel. Maybe you should, but you don't.

The record is bad. You conceived a plot, you engineered Paul King's first bit of luck, you introduced him to Tony Banks. Both were killed, and Konzakis, too, and Joe Gross ruined.

You tell yourself that it was, at the worst, manslaughter once removed. But it is past, and you have admitted it. No need to fight any more. You set the stage and from the wings the bad old gods moved remorselessly towards their victims.

So sometimes it is worth going back, even to Durrington.

At Elton, I picked up my wife and the two kids. And, since she will certainly be reading this, I say this to Jessie, there is more than one way of loving, and I think that Shirley was right, and I also think that working side by side in the publicity racket is a pretty good testing ground.

If now and then "a shadow remains," of somebody else, Jessie will understand. She, too, was in love, once, in a different way.